Amish Vows:

Amish
Heartbreaker

By Rose Doss

Book 3

ISBN: 9781983048579

Cover images courtesy of period images and canstockphoto
Cover by Joleene Naylor.

Manufactured/Produced in the United States

CHAPTER ONE

Standing at the buggy shop door next to Bishop Fisher's burly figure, Daniel Stoltzfus looked out through the cold dripping rain at Lydia Troyer—his boss' daughter—scurrying inside with the wash that had been hanging out on the line behind the *Haus*.

Lydia had grown up since he'd gone to school with her, just as, he supposed they all had.

"Daniel," the bishop said, "I know this time is difficult for you, but you did right by returning to a plain, simple life with *Gott*."

Daniel's lips quirked up on one side. "*Yah*, where I went wrong was to leave for the *Englischer* world in the first place."

The bishop's voice took on a scolding tone. "You know why you did that. You told me yourself. It was a mistaken lack of belief in yourself, *der Suh*. A moment of pride and confusion. *Gott* knows the heart though. You never doubted Him, but yourself."

Still idly watching Lydia's trim figure as she grappled with the basket of damp wash from the line, Daniel leaned back against the wide shop door frame. "Bishop Fisher, I know many here that look at me with a skeptical eye. It's understandable. My own *Eldre* now choose to leave their farm to my *Schweschder's* husband rather than to me, which was their original plan. I am...unreliable. At best, a *Bencil*. To be no longer trusted."

"*Der Suh*, you must not let this trouble you. The church elders have counseled with you. You have repented and now are again living a plain, simple life."

1

Stirring with discomfort, Daniel's words came out with a self-mocking tone in an attempt to hide his own deep guilt. "*Yah*, but some consider me a *Schlingel*. Particularly after I left both the church and the woman I was to marry."

"You are not a rogue, Daniel." The bishop slowly shook his head. "It takes a *Mann* of character to admit his wrong and I know, as do the other bishops, that returning to the church and to this community has been difficult. Particularly after your *Eldre* decided to leave the farm to your sister and her *Mann,* so you now must earn your keep working here in the buggy shop with Joel Troyer."

"What else could my *Eldre* do, Bishop? And I completely understand Mercy Yoder—who I was to marry—falling for Isaac Miller after I'd left her. Anyone can see they are very much in love."

The chilly autumn rain began drumming down more steadily, the scent of wet earth mingling pleasantly with the wood shavings and glue in the shop. Daniel continued to stare out at the water falling from the sky.

"Now that the crops have been harvested and the fields are fallow for the fall, they are to be married here soon, are they not?" The older *Mann* glanced at him, as if checking Daniel's reaction.

"*Yah*. Mercy's *Eldre* and many of her *Geschwischder* live here in Elizabethtown. After they marry here, I understand they will return to Mannheim where Isaac has a farm. I wish them the best. Mercy and I were never meant to marry."

The driving rain blanketed the yard between the *Haus* and Joel's shop, falling now in chilly gray sheets.

Daniel turned to look at the older *Mann* who'd walked by his side as Daniel made his amends upon his return from the *Englischer* world. "Even though I no longer have a farm, this life here is best for me. I am not discontented working with Joel. He's been very kind and his *familye* generous. I have a small room here beside the shop. Besides, I like working on buggies with Joel. He's a kind *Mann*, even tolerating me when I was an annoying *youngie*."

"But to work as a hired hand..." Bishop Fisher said mournfully.

"It is good work." Daniel smiled out at the rain. "And I've always liked buggies. Working on them is no hardship. Like I said, being back here is enough."

"That is as may be, Daniel," the bishop said enigmatically. "The greater issue now is to insert you again more fully into our community."

Staring sightlessly out the buggy shop door, he said. "The church members will eventually see that I mean my repentance."

"*Yah*. It will speed things up, however," the older *Mann* said bluntly, "if you take a good, steady *Frau*. A *Mann* with a *familye* is viewed as more settled down. More steady."

Daniel gave a barking laugh. "Bishop, after I left my previous fiancée within weeks of our planned wedding, no Amish woman will now—nor will her *Eldre* even allow her to—court with me."

The bishop squatted down in the shop doorway. "There are some..."

When Daniel looked a question down at him where he squatted next to him, the older *Mann* shifted some, not doing more than shooting an upward glance his way. "Some women...are not sought out by a lot of *Menner*. Their *familye* may try to help in this, but some still find no match."

Making no reply to this statement with its implication that there might be a woman desperate enough to marry him, Daniel kept his silence.

"Hagar Hershberger is courting with no one to my knowledge and hasn't ever." The bishop said, naming a single spinster who was at least eight years older than Daniel's twenty-two years.

He dug a stick in the edge of the puddle growing in front of the buggy shop. "Bishop...I cannot... I cannot see myself married to Hagar. I know her and she seems a fine woman, but.... I don't know what *Gott* would have me do. Despite all I've done, I want a *familye* and *Bopplis* of my own. But...not with Hagar."

"She is not that old," Bishop Fisher pointed out, his defense of the woman made in a weak tone.

"*Neh*, but I don't think she's the woman for me." Daniel drew a deep breath. "The road I've taken has been difficult and will likely continue that way for a while. I cannot see sharing it with her."

The older *Mann* rose from his crouched position, his gaze not wavering.

Feeling a wave a gratitude that he'd found such grace in his community, Daniel concluded. "I do not easily ask any woman to share this road."

"Naomi." Later after their midday meal, Lydia shifted a washed, sudsy plate to her younger sister as they stood at their *Eldre's* sink overlooking the chilly gray yard, the rain still drumming. "Here...and tell me more about life as a married *Frau*."

She prodded the conversation along, hoping to keep herself from going over and over the thoughts in her head of her own predicament. These hadn't yet led to any good decision.

"It is *gut*, sister." Blonde, blue-eyed Naomi flashed her a pretty smile.

"It was generous of you and Jethro to come have lunch with us." Lydia absently passed her washrag over another plate. "I know he must be relieved to have finished the summer work and take some time to relax now that autumn is blowing in."

"He is. It was nice that his *Daed* and *Bruders* carved out such a big piece of farmland from theirs for us, but it does keep him busy in the growing season."

"*Yah*". Lydia frowned down at the water, unable to totally push back the regrets that crept into her thoughts, her head filled with despair and guilt. *If only... If only...* What had she been thinking?

"Is something bothering you?" Naomi hissed the words quietly, as the door closed behind their *Eldre* and Jethro who were heading out to the shop to examine the buggies her *Daed* was building with his new hire.

Lydia knew they had gone, but she looked around the empty kitchen area anyway. She felt so horrible about her predicament. So bad and wrong. Admitting even to her younger sister seemed impossible...although the truth could not be hidden for long. "What do you mean?"

"Only that you are distracted," Naomi said, "and that usually means you have something big on your mind. Spill it!"

"Whatever do you mean?" Lydia scrubbed harder at the plate in her hands, staring blindly at the sudsy water.

Her sister reached over to stop the movement of her hand, prompting Lydia to look over at her.

"Tell me," Naomi commanded, "we are alone. There is no one else to hear if that's what keeps you silent. You are not given to keeping surprises."

"I can't imagine what you mean." She looked blankly out the window at the rain. Naomi, although three years younger and the last child in the *familye,* had always been Lydia's confidant more than their eldest sister, Grace, but Lydia had no idea how to share this secret with her sister.

"*Schweschder*. Tell me!"

Lydia kept her gaze on the drops trickling down the window, absently noting Daniel Stoltzfus' fit form—now her *Daed's* new hired man—walking out of the buggy shop with Bishop Fisher, seeming impervious to the damp.

It seemed a decade since they'd gone to school together.

Naomi tugged on her apron, as she'd done since childhood, but Lydia didn't respond. Her secret was too terrible to tell. Many *youngies* did risky, bad things on *rumspringa*—smoking, drinking and running wild—but most didn't bring this kind of dilemma home with them. Maybe a lightning bolt would kill her and she wouldn't bring shame to her family.

Lydia infused cheerfulness in her voice, changing the subject, "So, is Abe going to plant fall crops? *Neh*, I imagine it's too late for that."

Suddenly, she realized her cheeks were damp with tears and she quickly lifted a hand from Naomi's clasp to scrub the back across her face to hide this.

"*Schweschder,*" Naomi's voice lowered in awed quietness, her hand still clasping Lydia's other hand in the sink, "why are you crying?"

"I cannot tell you!" Lydia sobbed softly now. "I cannot."

"Did something happen on your *rumspringa*? I know you only returned to Elizabethtown a week ago, after taking *rumspringa* at an older age than most. Are you alright?"

Lydia hung her head, bending forward toward the sink, sobs making her shoulders tremble no matter how she resisted. Her *Mamm* could walk back into the room any moment. Although her secret could not be kept much longer, she shrank from exposing it to her *Eldre*.

"I never thought you should go work in that restaurant. In that town where we know no one," her younger sister said in a scolding voice. "What happened? Come and tell me. Get your hands out of the dishwater and sit at the table."

Naomi pressed her into a chair at the table where they'd gathered for lunch. "Did someone there at the restaurant hurt you?"

"*Neh.* I mean, *yah*, I'm upset over something that happened on *rumspringa*, but *neh*, no one there hurt me. Not in the way you mean."

"Well, what did happen?" Naomi sounded affronted. "You aren't crying over nothing!"

"I made some bad choices, Naomi. I—I'm terrible." Her mouth felt full of ashes as she spoke the bitter words.

Naomi snorted. "You? You are the good *Dochder*, the one our *Eldre* have never had to worry about. Grace and I have often remarked on it."

Lydia drew in a shuddering breath, plastering on a smile she knew was pathetic.

Naomi had spent her own brief *rumspringa* weeks working with Abe's cousin in a nearby town. Lydia didn't think her sister had done much during that time that she couldn't have done here at home, returning quickly to join the church and marry her long-time sweetie the previous autumn.

So much for her being a troublesome child.

"I cannot tell you. You just wouldn't understand, Naomi." The words escaped her in a despairing wail.

Starting to look alarmed, her sister asked, "What did you do in Bedford, Lydia? Kill someone? You didn't have an accident in an *Englischer* car or drive over someone in a buggy, did you?"

Despite her despair, Naomi's wild guess surprised a watery chuckle from Lydia. "*Neh.* I didn't kill anyone. Is that the best you can come up with?"

"It is more likely that you did nothing horrible. As I said, you are the good sister."

"Not anymore, Naomi," she admitted after a moment. "I have sinned. Terribly. I-I laid with an *Englischer…*"

Not looking up, her side view told Lydia her sister's mouth had fallen open. "…and I think I am now pregnant with his child."

Naomi straightened in her chair, the color draining from her complexion. She leaned forward, putting her hand over her sister's. "Oh, Lydia."

Later that evening, Lydia sat at the wide kitchen table eating supper with her *Daed*, her *Mamm* and Daniel Stoltzfus.

"This is such a good meal, Lydia" her *Mamm* said, dipping into the soup. "Your *Daed* and I are so fortunate that you are still with us. The other children have already married and left us."

Her *Mamm* continued, carefully swirling around her spoon in her bowl. "There will be several weddings at the service this Sunday. I wonder if you, Daniel, will go."

The older woman sent a swift, speculative glance in his direction. "I've heard that your former fiancée, Mercy Yoder, is to say vows with Isaac Miller."

A flash of embarrassment went over Lydia at her *Mamm's* tactless statement.

In the middle of taking a spoonful of the soup, Daniel paused, lifting his gaze to her *Mamm*. "*Yah*, I will go, *Frau* Troyer. I wish Isaac and Mercy nothing, but good. Isaac's *Bruder*, Enoch, and his *Frau* Kate are here to witness it, as is a young woman, a relative of Kate Miller's, I believe."

"Now, *Mamm*," Joel Troyer chided, apparently as embarrassed as Lydia by her *Mamm's* tactless question. "There is no reason for Daniel not to wish Isaac and Mercy well. He's following his own path to a plain, simple life and this no longer includes this Mercy."

Acutely aware of her *Mamm's* thoughtless words, Lydia sent a brief apologetic smile toward Daniel. "*Daed*, how do crops go on my *Bruders'* farms? Are they all glad to have chosen to be farmers instead of making buggies like you?"

"They both seem very happy to be where they are," her *Daed* said in a dry voice. "None of them has much interest in buggy-making, despite all the afternoons they helped in my shop. Bart, in particular, seems born to be a farmer. You remember, Miriam, how he always snuck off to help his *Onkle* Stoltzfus, your *Bruder*?"

Joel Troyer laughed. "He used to just disappear without saying a word."

Lydia's *Mamm* chuckled at the memory, her girth shaking. "*Yah*, as though we ever minded his working with his *Onkle*."

"And then Adam went to help Bart on the land and found his own calling," Joel concluded comfortably.

"It is kind of you," Daniel sent her *Daed* a faint smile, "to be happy for them both when neither wished to take on your business."

This new, quiet Daniel seemed more perceptive than most. He seemed different somehow after his time in the *Englischer* world. Lydia looked at him with approval while Joel responded mildly that he'd never wanted his sons to follow in footsteps that weren't right for them.

"Can I get you more soup, Daniel?" she asked as she rose from the table.

"*Yah. Denki.* It's very good."

Lydia felt herself flushing with pleasure again as she reached for his bowl. "Then let me get you more."

Over a week later, Daniel stood next to a buggy, yanking on the broken wheel with Abel Schrock, the younger *Mann* that sometimes also helped in Joel's buggy shop. Because Daniel was a little older and had been several grades ahead of Abel in school, he hadn't really spent much time with him before.

"*Yah*. Grab hold of it there," Daniel instructed, bracing a foot against the buggy's springs as he and Abel jointly yanked to pull free the broken wheel.

"Whew!" Abel muttered, stopping briefly to wipe his hands on his pants. "This is a gut-buster. If only those spokes had held as well as this wheel."

"Come on, Abel!" Daniel said through gritted teeth as he continued struggling with the wheel. "We can do this."

Shifting around to both grab different sides, they worked together at getting it off. They finally tugged the circle free, having to wiggle it in spots.

While they stood gathering their breath, the wheel then on the floor in front of them, Abel motioned to Joel's office with his head. "Isn't that Mercy Yoder in there with the *Mann* ordering a buggy?"

"*Yah*. She's *Frau* Miller now, though." Daniel used a bandana to wipe bead of sweat off his face. "She and Isaac, the *Mann* she married just this last Sunday, will live in Mannheim."

"Oh, that's right," Abel grinned. "I knew I recognized them from somewhere. They were one of the couples who got married in church this last week."

"They were." Daniel hefted the now-free buggy wheel onto the worktable.

Abel helped him shift up to lie on the flat surface and picked up a tool to start working loose one broken spoke while Daniel worked to free the jagged section of another one. He threw Daniel a curious look. "Weren't you and *Frau* Miller an item before?

Seems like I remember seeing you together a lot and...weren't you two published to marry last fall?"

"*Yah*, we were," Daniel focused on further loosening the spoke, "but we parted ways and Mercy ended up marrying Isaac."

It was only natural that those in the community were curious. He figured it was a matter of time before Abel asked about Daniel's having left for the *Englischer* world. He wasn't looking forward to discussing that.

The younger man now grinned good-naturedly and waggled his eyebrows. "That Mercy's a nice-looking—"

"Isaac Miller's *Frau*." Daniel inserted, biting back an answering smile. He didn't think Abel meant any disrespect. "It isn't *gut* that you should finish that remark, I think, young Abel."

"Probably true," Abel agreed, still smiling down at the wheel on which he worked.

Just then another buggy drove into the yard in front of Joel's shop. Drawn by the sound of the wheels, Daniel looked up from his task. Since Joel was busy in his shop office, Daniel walked over to the buggy, seeing Bishop Fisher's burly figure at the reins.

"*Goedemorgen*, Bishop." It was then Daniel noticed a sullen-looking boy of about thirteen on the other side of his friend. "Oh, I didn't see you. *Goedemorgen*, Mark."

"This *kleinzoon* of mine is reluctantly running errands with me since he can't get along with his *Geschwischder* and his *Mamm* is at her wits end." Bishop Fisher raised his eyebrows as he looked over at the boy. "So he's spending the afternoon with his *Grossdaddi* instead."

"I didn't always get along with my brothers and sisters, either," Daniel confessed in a quiet voice. "Is there something I can get for you Bishop?"

The boy in the buggy sat silently beside his grandfather, the sullen expression still on his face, his broad straw hat seeming too large for his scrawny neck.

"*Yah*, some *schaviut* took the reflector off my buggy and I need to get a new one. *Youngies*."

"You do," agreed Daniel, shooting another look at Mark, huddled next to Bishop Fisher. "Driving without one is illegal, not to mention dangerous. Let me get it for you. I believe I know where Joel stores them."

His back turned while he looked through the cabinet where the reflectors were stored, he heard Lydia greeting the Bishop. "...and I see young Mark is with you."

"*Goedemorgan*, Miss Lydia," the boy said in an awkward, shy voice.

His greeting to her was made in such a different tone that Daniel looked around as his hand closed on the reflector.

"*Goedemorgan* to you, too. Are you running errands with your *Grossdaddi*?" A large white tea cup in her hand, she smiled at the pre-adolescent boy.

"*Yah*," Mark responded, blushing at her attention.

"Here you are, Bishop." Daniel came back to the buggy, still grinning at the thought that an attractive woman had this effect on *Menner* of any age. And Lydia with her smiling brown eyes and slender figure definitely counted as an attractive woman.

"Excuse me, Bishop and *Youngie* Mark. I must get this to *Daed* while it's still hot." She smiled at them and at Daniel before disappearing into the shop office.

With her departure, Daniel noted the sullen expression again descended onto the boy's face.

"Here you are, Bishop." He handed the reflector to the older *Mann*. "If you'll wait just a moment, I'll attach it for you."

"Thank you! That would be kindly of you, Daniel." Bishop Fisher beamed. "I accept your offer."

"Hold on. I'll get a screwdriver." He disappeared into the shop where Abel had picked out the wheel spokes and was measuring several against the others to see which fit best.

"Looks like Joel's *Dochder* brought him some tea," Abel commented with lifted, wiggling brows as Daniel sifted through the drawer in which the screwdrivers were held.

"Young Abel," he murmured, "are you courting with a specific *Maedel*?"

"*Neh*," the younger *Mann* admitted with a smile. "I usually drive one or the other home from Sings, but my *Daed* thinks I'm still too young to know who'd be best for me."

"He's definitely right about that." Daniel selected a screwdriver, shutting the drawer. "And let me recommend you be careful that the *Maedels* you drive home know it."

Abel laughed as Daniel took the tool and some screws back to the Bishop's buggy.

Screwing the replacement reflector to it, he made no comment when Lydia reappeared, bearing several empty cups from her father's office. He heard her goodbyes to the two waiting in the buggy and as she walked behind it to head into the *Haus*, she grinned at him.

"We certainly can't pray to *Gott* to have someone steal the reflectors off more buggies," Lydia commented in a lowered voice, the wicked smile still on her face, "but just think of the business we'd get if more were to be taken."

Continuing to twist the screwdriver as she mounted the steps that led to the *Haus*, Daniel shook his head, the corner of his mouth lifting. Lydia Troyer had a bad girl streak.

When Daniel looked up from his work as the afternoon waned, he was surprised to see Lydia Troyer's trim figure hesitating in the wide buggy shop door.

Knowing Joel wasn't there, Daniel asked, "Is there something I can help you with, *Maedel* Lydia?"

Peering around the shop, she held a full laundry basket propped on her hip. Bringing her fine brown eyes back to meet his gaze she finally asked, "This chilly showery weather is making things difficult. Is Able not here? I thought he could help me a moment."

"*Neh*. Joel took Abel on an errand with him." Daniel reached down for the last nut to go on the buggy wheel. "I'm here alone for the moment."

"Dang." Lydia remained standing indecisively in the door before glancing back at the weak slanting afternoon light that now gleamed through the shop windows and backlit her in the doorway. Although it had again rained all morning with the cooler fall weather, the clouds had just lifted to allow the sun to peek through before setting on the horizon.

Slipping the nut onto the last wheel bolt, he cast her another sideways look. "Is there anything I can do to help?"

She looked back at him, considering. "Is this a rush job you're doing on the buggy? Is anyone waiting for it?"

Daniel cleaned his fingers on a nearby work rag, a corner of his mind lifting in amusement at question. She clearly had something in mind. "Not that I know. Do you need my help?"

"Well, I had thought to have Able help, but the afternoon sun is already starting to fade." She gestured toward the basket. "And these sheets are still wet."

He cocked an eyebrow at her. "*Maedel* Lydia, are you asking me to hang out laundry?"

"I am," she said with a saucy smile. "If it's not beneath you."

"I cannot see how bedding is beneath anyone. We all want dry sheets to sleep on a night," he responded matter-of-factly. "Do you think you have time for them to dry on the line?"

"Yes," she said practically. "Sheets dry quickly. I would have gotten them out earlier, but there was rain and then the cold cloudy weather wouldn't have allowed for drying."

Daniel put the work rag on the nearby work bench. "Then we'd better get to it."

Following Lydia out of the buggy shop through the yard to the line, he stopped as she set down the basket. "*Maedel*, I must admit to never having hung out laundry before."

A smile broke over her face like sunlight over water. "Not even with your *Mamm* when you were a *Scholar*?"

His sisters had undoubtedly done this. Daniel knew he'd been sheltered from some tasks, maybe too much, even by his grim *Daed*. Maybe if he hadn't, he'd have been more realistic about life. Reflecting briefly that it did no good to blame his *Eldre's* actions

13

for his missteps, he grinned back, inviting her, *"Neh,* I didn't do it even then. Show me, please."

She hauled up a hunk of wet material from the rush basket on the damp ground, draping the sheet over the line. "Like this."

With efficient moves, she pulled the wide material up to hang halfway across the line, pulling wooden clothes pins from her capacious apron pockets.

"You have clearly done this before." Daniel reached into the basket for another sheet. "I just put it over the clothes line?"

Another laugh bubbled out of her as she reached over to twitch straight a wrinkled portion of the sheet. *"Yah.* Like that. Here. Have some clothes pins to pinch it with to make sure it doesn't fall off the line."

She handed him several and he wrestled to fasten the wooden pin over the wet sheet, the maneuver unaccustomed. "Ummm."

Lydia had taken another sheet to the parallel line. Slipping a pin dexterously over another sheet, she said, "Here, let me show you."

She stretched over to push down more firmly the clothes pin he held and he found himself uncomfortably aware of how the fabric of her dress pulled tightly across her chest. Lydia was a comely woman, but he didn't need to focus on that now.

"I will soon be trained to do all the work around here," he forced himself to say naturally. "You'd think being able to put a wheel on a buggy would make this easier."

Just then a breeze kicked up unexpectedly, blowing up the damp corner of the sheet with which he was wrestling over the line and it landed across his face with a slap. With his hands held out in the act of pulling the wet sheet over the line, he stopped when the fabric flapped over his head, clinging there.

Hearing the sudden peal of Lydia's laughter at his predicament, Daniel found himself laughing behind the sheet fold. *"Maedel.* My hands being occupied, do you think you could help?"

"Of course," she said in a giggle-choked voice as she freed him.

In that instant, his hands holding the wet sheet to the line as a still-laughing Lydia appeared when she took the sheet from his face, the thought streaked across Daniel's mind that *Gott* had put him in just the right place.

CHAPTER TWO

Walking into the worship meeting with her *Mamm* several days later, Lydia Troyer was too aware of Daniel following behind her with her *Daed*. It was silly to be so conscious of his gaze on her backside. Particularly since it might not even be there.

Ever since her afternoon adventure with Daniel at the clothes line, she could no longer think of him as just a *Mann* with whom she'd gone to school years back.

Pushing aside the memory, she found her *Mamm* a seat in the crowded *Haus* and moved on to sit at the next section of seats in the main room where an empty chair sat to the side. It was hard not to think of her dilemma—or to let herself dwell on more pleasant thoughts of the childhood acquaintance with the strong masculine form who now worked with her *Daed* in the buggy shop.

When an elderly woman came down the aisle between the chairs, Lydia welcomed the distraction, springing up.

"Hello, *Frau* Bieler! Please take this seat. I can find another and the breeze from that window should be cool, but not too chilly."

Lydia smiled at the aged woman as she assisted her frail form to sit in the comfy chair.

"Thank you, dear. That is so sweet of you," *Frau* Bieler quavered, bobbing her white-*kapped* head as she situated herself. "But where will you sit?"

The older woman peered around doubtfully. "It is getting so crowded already."

16

"*Yah*, it is," agreed Lydia, "but I see an open seat next to my sister, Naomi. Don't you worry. I'll find a seat."

Leaving *Frau* Bieler waving a frail hand of gratitude at her, Lydia made her way through the crowded room. To her relief, she didn't feel queasy this morning. Maybe she was wrong and her sin would have no physical consequence.

Maybe, maybe.

Crossing the room towards her *Schweschder*, Lydia stopped beside Mercy Miller, still in Elizabethtown while Joel and Daniel finished the ordered buggy. Having gone to school with Mercy as well as Daniel, she greeted her easily, squatting in front of the *Boppli* on the lap of a *Frau* who sat next to Mercy.

Nodding to the women, Lydia offered the *Boppli* a finger, her heart constricting as the child clasped firmly in her chubby hand.

"Hello, *Boppli*." Lydia smiled at the babe.

Everything was wrong about a child coming into the world from an unmarried Amish girl after she consorted with an *Englischer*, but…Lydia couldn't keep from softening at the thought of holding her own *Boppli*.

The little girl stared at her solemnly, her tiny black *kapp* framing a fair baby face with intense unsmiling blue eyes, her sweet little fingers still locked around Lydia's.

"She's a little shy of all these new faces," commented her *Mamm*, jiggling her knees a little to entertain the babe.

"Lydia," Mercy said, "this is my friend, Kate. Her husband, Enoch, is my Isaac's *Bruder*. And this beside Kate is Anna Lehmann, a relative of hers. Anna was kind enough to accompany us all here for the wedding and she will stay here a while with my *Mamm*."

"Nice to meet you, Anna and Kate." Lydia smiled and nodded at them both, not ignoring the younger Anna. "And this wonderful little bundle is--?"

"Elizabeth Miller," her *Mamm* beamed, again jiggling the *Boppli* a little on her knees. "She's named for my mother who is no longer with us."

"That's a lovely name, little Elizabeth." Lydia included the two women, asking, "How long do you stay before you must head home. Are you leaving as soon as my *Daed* finishes the new buggy?"

Kate laughed. "*Yah*, Enoch, I and Anna have tagged along with Mercy and Isaac on their wedding visits long enough. We go back soon, while Anna stays here for a visit.."

"We don't mind having you drive with us and you know my *Mamm* is thrilled to have little Elizabeth to spoil. You just want to get home to your Sarah."

"My older *Dochder*," Kate told Lydia. "And, *yah*. We do miss her. She's staying with friends, but it's soon time for us all to be home together. I know Anna's *Mamm* will eventually be glad to get her back, too, when she finished her stay here with Mercy's *familye*."

Lydia chuckled, smiling at the woman. "I completely understand. How old is this other *Dochder*?"

Kate shook her head ruefully. "She's just turned ten and I can't believe how grown up she is."

"Sarah is a wonderful *Maedel*," Anna spoke up to confirm. "Still a *Scholar*, but acting like a *Mamm* to little Elizabeth."

The crowd began to quiet down as Bishop Fisher came to the front.

"I must find a seat!" Lydia said in a whisper voice, giving the *Boppli* a finger wave. "Nice to meet you all!"

Receiving a quiet goodbye from Mercy and the two women, Lydia made her way toward her sister as soundlessly as she could. As their church services were always held in members' homes and were usually very crowded, her path toward Naomi was indirect.

"This way," whispered Hagar Hershberger as Lydia sidled down a row past her. "I think it's clearer to go over there."

"*Denki*," Lydia grinned her thanks at the woman. Hagar was a good ten years older than her, but she'd been friendly in school, even towards the younger group of *Kinder*. Now that both she and Hagar were grown, single women, Lydia liked the woman even more. She knew what many said about the other woman, calling

Hagar a spinster, but Lydia privately respected the thirty year-old woman for refusing to marry where her heart did not sing.

At least, that was what Hagar had indicated once.

If Lydia only faced that option now. Her situation was much, much worse. Slinking as quietly as possible toward the empty seat next to her sister, Lydia's thoughts ran ahead of her.

No matter how hard she hoped that this wasn't happening, she couldn't fool herself any longer, even though the queasiness was less this morning. The problem was real. She didn't have any good choices—having stupidly put herself and the coming *Boppli* at peril. The little seed she was now convinced grew inside her made the whole situation different. After much thought, she knew she needed to confess to and confer with Bishop Fisher.

He would help her see what *Gott* would have her do now.

She dreaded telling her *Mamm* and *Daed*, though. It would be so much harder than telling Naomi. Lydia knew her *Eldre* would be heart-broken.

The next day, Lydia went out to the buggy shop around noon, the banging, clanking sounds there familiar after all these years. What wasn't as familiar was seeing Daniel Stoltzfus' sweaty, powerful figure in the place of the aged shop assistant who used to work for her *Daed*. The elderly Hiram had never had such broad shoulders or looked so good banging on a carriage wheel and had certainly never caused Lydia's heart to shift into a self-conscious pitter-patter.

A smile twitched at her lips, remembering the damp sheet blown across Daniel's face.

Her *Daed's* former worker, Hiram had retired not long ago, which left Joel Troyer looking for another assistant. That he'd also found a part-time assistant in Abel Schrock was *gut* for both her *Daed* and Daniel, as the buggy shop had grown.

As Lydia walked past to call *Daed* in for his lunch, she grinned to herself at the thought that in hiring Daniel, *Daed* had certainly improved the look of the shop. Not that the plain, simple people were directed to look on the outside, but it would be ridiculous to deny that Daniel's outside wasn't significantly different than the kindly Hiram and even better than young Abel.

Lydia trod over to the shop, sticking her head inside. "*Daed,* lunch is ready."

Her father looked up from the board where he'd pinned line drawings of the different buggies that had been ordered. "*Denki, Dochder.* Tell Daniel to come in, as well. Abel has gone home early today, but we should feed Daniel."

"Okay," she agreed, not displeased to invite the *Mann* in for lunch. It would be interesting to see if she could work the damp sheet episode into the conversation and get the normally-taciturn worker to crack a smile. Lydia grinned at the thought.

Half an hour later, her *Daed* and Daniel having sluiced themselves clean under the pump in the yard, the two sat at the table with her *Mamm* and Lydia.

"You seem busy in the shop," Lydia remarked, spooning some green beans onto her *Daed's* and then Daniel's plates after having served her *Mamm.*

"*Yah,* we are most days," *Daed* confirmed. "Even more now that Daniel's friends from Mannheim have ordered a buggy."

Lydia speared a green bean from her own plate, asking Daniel, "And they wait for it to drive it back there?"

He responded with a half-smile in her direction, "*Yah.* I believe so. *Frau* Miller knows your *Daed's* good work."

"It's understandable, since Mercy grew up here," Miriam Troyer remarked, her white *kapp* bobbing as she spoke.

"How did they get here without a buggy? Lydia asked. "I thought I saw Kate's husband driving one the other day."

Daniel said in a calm and deliberate voice, "*Yah.* Isaac Miller's *Bruder,* and his *Frau* drove with a young relative of hers here for their wedding."

"Oh, that's right! Anna, Kate and her *Bobbli.* I met them at the service yesterday," Lydia exclaimed, connecting the dots.

"*Dochder*," Miriam said, changing the subject, "would you wait on returning to your sewing to bring the pickling barrel in from the storage area? We're running low on pickles and you know how your *Daed* loves them."

"I do," confirmed Joel, chuckling. "Particularly your pickles, wife."

Miriam turned pink, smiling at his affectionate remark.

"*Yah, Mamm.* I'll do it right after I clean up." Lydia was accustomed to seeing this kind of interaction between her *Eldre*. She noted that across the table, the corners of Daniel lips also lifted, his quiet smile confirming that he'd noted her father's compliment.

"I can bring it in, Lydia."

She looked up in surprise at Daniel's offer. With the buggy shop so busy, she hadn't expected them to have the time.

"It's in the storage area back where the extra buggy bodies sit?" he asked, his blue eyes seeking her for confirmation.

"There's no need for you to bother and take time from your work." She sent a twinkling glance his way. "I assure you I am quite strong enough to carry in a medium-size pickle barrel."

As if responding to the teasing note in her words, the corner of his mouth lifted again. "It's not a bother. I'll put it on the back porch."

"*Denki.*" She smiled back. "There may be several barrels in the shed, but—"

"I'm sure the vinegar smell will direct me to the correct one," he retorted.

"It will," she agreed, grinning.

After lunch, the two *Menner,* having this time, washed up at the kitchen sink before returning to the shop, Daniel paused beside a quilt frame that was tilted now against a wall.

"Yours?" He cocked an eye at Lydia.

She ducked her head, not sure why she felt shy about this. "*Yah.*"

"*Gott* has given you a talent." He said simply in his quiet way. "It looks warm and soft."

She smiled. "I like needlework. I always have. *Daed* and *Mamm* have me make all their clothes."

"Mmmm." He kept looking at the quilt in her frame. "I can see why. Who is this for? You or your *Mamm* and *Daed*?"

"It's actually for my younger sister, Naomi. She just married last year and she and her husband, Jethro, are still collecting bedding."

Daniel shot her a look. "Jethro Wyse?"

"*Yah*. You remember he was a year or so younger than us?"

"I do remember." Daniel's voice was as dry as his face was expressionless. "He was a pest."

His comment surprised a ripple of laughter from her. "That he was when a *youngie*, but Naomi seems to find him to her taste now. Even to the rest of us, he's not so bad."

Replacing the broad straw hat on his head, Daniel said in an even tone. "I'm sure this is a relief to you all. I'll put that pickle barrel on the back porch."

"I appreciate it." Still chuckling, she watched him head out the back door of the *Haus*.

After his desertion of Mercy Yoder just before they were to marry—and his having left the church altogether for the *Englischer* world—Lydia knew Daniel wasn't viewed by many in their community as a good risk.

An Amish heartbreaker.

He had certainly broken Mercy Yoder's heart when he left and that only made his return to their life watched with even greater skepticism. Still, he made Lydia laugh, she found, and that alone made her consider him less suspiciously. Really, how many *Menner* would agree to help with hanging out the laundry?

After all, she was in no position to judge others' sins.

Looking out the window over the kitchen sink as she washed up after lunch, she couldn't help see how hard Daniel worked with her *Daed*...and notice how he sweated through the single worn shirt he wore. He must wash it nightly because he never smelled bad.

22

Her gaze dropping to the suds in the sink water, Lydia drew in a deep breath and let it out slowly. Making a shirt for her father's assistant would at least keep her mind off the troubling reality she knew she soon must face.

The next morning, Daniel stood in the doorway of his small room, staring down at Lydia's determined face. "What do you mean you're here to measure me for a new shirt?"

She calmly moved forward and he fell back, allowing her into the room. "You need another one—probably several more—since you've been wearing the same one every day. It's getting so worn its practically see-through."

"*Neh.*" He felt thrown off balance, flustered in this new sensation. "I am fine. I don't need anything."

She dropped her folded hands—which held a swath of sturdy, practical-looking white fabric—against her skirt. "Daniel Stoltzfus, do you deny that you have only the one shirt?"

"*Neh*, I don't deny it," he responded, feeling even more ruffled, "but its fine. I don't need more. I just rinse this one."

She yawned, shifting her hold on the fabric to reach up and scratch her shoulder. "Every night you wash it, don't you? And then hang it to dry? This isn't a good use of your time—"

He opened his mouth to protest further, feeling strange at having this young woman provide him with clothing.

"...time my *Daed* counts on you to help him in the buggy shop."

Daniel stopped. There was really nothing to say to that.

"This will only take a moment." She'd put the fabric down on his bed and now held up a worn fabric measuring tape. "Come. Turn around. I make all our clothing. It will be nothing."

Reluctantly, Daniel slowly turned around, tensing with the strangeness of it all. Even though they'd hung out wet sheets together, having her here in his room was strange. He could feel her behind him, her hands warm as she held the tape measure to his

23

shoulders and down the length of his arms. His sisters or his *Mamm* had always made his clothes before. People who were familiar to him.

Of course, those connections were all broken since he'd run off to the *Englischer* world and hadn't mended much with his return, although he had hopes.

It was beyond bizarre to have Lydia here in his small sleeping room with him. Just the two of them alone. Her stretching to reach around him with the measuring tape. He'd never thought of being measured as disturbing before.

He'd returned to his Amish life—knowing he'd broken hearts by leaving. Mercy's. His *Eldre's*. But there was no other place that felt more like home for him. His life, he knew now, wasn't in the *Englischer* world. He'd once thought that facing his fears of that world would make him feel more brave and stronger, but he hadn't felt stronger there, even though he had survived.

Coming back to this life, that was where he found the need for courage.

"Turn." Lydia Troyer ran her tape measure from his shoulder to below his waist. Daniel took a breath and stared resolutely ahead.

"I'm not going to attack you," she said with a tremor of amusement in her voice as she wrote his measurements on the scrap of paper beneath her pencil.

"I know that," he retorted.

"As I said, I've made clothes for my sisters and *Bruders*. My *Eldre*, too. If you're this uncomfortable being measured, it's a good thing I'm not making you pants."

"I'm sure you're very *gut* at it. A gift from *Gott*," he said as politely as he could, deliberately making his tone level, even though he'd flushed a little at her comment and at the thought of that intimacy.

"It's not a matter of being *gut* at it, but of keeping the wearer clean and comfortable." She picked up the fabric that had sat on his bedstead, looking around the small room as she did. "You are very tidy."

"*Yah*." Daniel had no idea why he felt defensive about this. He'd always liked things straight around him, even as a child. There was nothing wrong with that. Something about this young woman unsettled him.

Lydia made a wry face at him. "It is not always so with *Menner*. Some girls, too, do not keep things tidy."

He had no idea why she made him so jumpy. Lydia was a small thing and had never been anything other than friendly to him. It was also not to be denied that she was a nice looking girl. Round where *Gott* made women round and slender...

In an awkward voice, he tried to follow her conversational lead. "*Yah*, not all are concerned with this."

"Well, I should have these ready in no time," she briskly promised, again shifting her armful.

Noticing that her breathing suddenly quickened and that she seemed to have gone a faint shade of green, he said, "There is no hurry. Are you alright?"

"*Yah*," she responded in a suddenly suffocated voice. "I just need to leave. Right now. I'll let you know when the shirts are finished."

To his surprise, she rushed out of his small room.

Daniel stared after her. One moment, she'd been teasing him and the next she acted as if she couldn't get away quickly enough. It was all very puzzling.

Two days later, Lydia bent over the garden fence, retching as though her toenails were coming up. Caught up in the rebellion of her stomach, she didn't immediately notice the legs of the *Mann* who came to stand beside her.

"Are you all right, Lydia?"

In the ungraceful position of hanging over the fence, she wiped the back of her hand across a mouth that tasted of regret and disgrace. It could not be long now. She would have to tell the truth.

"Lydia?"

She flashed a glance over and saw that as she feared, Daniel stood beside her. If only it had been anyone but him. She felt the heat climb from her chest into her neck and cheeks.

"You are ill. Shall I fetch your *Mamm*?"

She turned quickly then, saying in a beseeching voice. "*Neh*, Daniel. I'm fine. I'll be…fine."

Under the shade of his broad hat brim, she saw him frown. "But you were sick. I heard you."

"*Neh*," she felt her cheeks heat and shook her head again. "I am not sick. Not anymore. I feel better now. The…meat we had for lunch must have been bad. There is no need to get anyone."

Daniel frowned at her. "But we all ate dinner together. It did not taste spoiled."

She quickly wiped her mouth again, stepping back from the garden fence in hope that she could leave her embarrassing moment as easily and that the smell of vomit hadn't reached him. "I—I must have gotten a part that the rest of you didn't eat. I—I thought it tasted a little spoiled. I should have said something. I'm glad—"

She swallowed hard as he followed her away from the garden. "—glad it poisoned no one else."

He looked at her, his gaze searching her face when she came to a stop outside the buggy shop.

"You have been in the storage shed?" Lydia infused her voice with a brightness she didn't feel. "It's good I introduced you to it when you went for the pickle barrel."

"*Yah*."

She felt his continued stare.

"Are you sure you're not sick?"

"Oh, I'm sure," Lydia responded immediately, keeping her bitterness about this to herself. "I'm sure."

.

CHAPTER THREE

"You what?" Her *Mamm* sank into a chair at the table in the late afternoon a day later. "On your *rumspringa*? With an *Englischer*?"

Joel Troyer just stared at Lydia, dismay spreading over his features as he said mournfully, "Oh, *Dochder*."

Having just confessed the news, Lydia bent her head over the table, tears blurring the table cloth in front of her. "I have spoken with Bishop Fisher…and prayed for *Gott's* forgiveness. Many times. Such a horrible mistake, *Daed*."

"And you are with child?" Her *Mamm* seemed near to tears herself. "With child!"

Lydia's heart broke all over again, seeing her *Mamm* drop her head into worn hands. "It's going to be okay, *Mamm*. Don't cry."

"And unmarried. You are unmarried, but with child. And by an *Englischer*!" Her mother wrung her hands, continuing to weep as if Lydia hadn't spoken. "*Dochder*. Oh, *Dochder*. How can the bishop help with that?"

"It will be alright." Joel seemed both resigned and staunch. "You are part of us. We all make mistakes. You have spoken to the bishop. It is *Gott's* way to forgive, so must we."

"It cannot be alright!" wailed her *Mamm*. "You should have married Peter Stromeyer when he wanted to court with you. Why did you have to take your *rumspringa* in a town away from all our relatives? You should have stayed closer."

"*Mamm*," Joel Troyer pulled his wife into a sustaining hug. "*Mamm*, we will handle this. We will stick with Lydia and handle this."

"I don't see how." Her shoulders shook as she sobbed. "My Lydia! You have always been such a *gut* girl! You should go now to old Peter Stromeyer! I think he's still unmarried."

"*Mamm*," Lydia said in a low, strained voice. "I—I cannot marry Peter. You know he is older than *Daed* and only looking for a wife to care for him now that he's sick!"

"It doesn't matter," Miriam gabbled out. "He may be old and sick, but at least you'd be married when you have this *Boppli*!"

"You said you have spoken to the bishop?" Her Daed's voice was heavy, obviously laden with worry.

She felt so horrible for a moment Lydia wished she were dead. To bring such shame to her *familye* all for that one heedless, lonely, mistaken moment. "*Yah*. I also told Naomi. I've spoken to Bishop Fisher about this. Several times. He—he told me *Gott* still loved me. And that I should remember to rejoice in the *Boppli* as a gift."

Her *Mamm* wailed loudly at these words. "Not if you don't marry Peter Stromeyer!"

Lydia flinched at the sound. Joel then pulled her into his arms. "We will come through this storm, *Dochder*. You will see…and I believe the bishop may be right."

"I do love this little *Boppli*, Daed." She pressed her face into her *Daed's* warm neck, the comforting familiar smell sifting through her as her tears fell.

They sat this way as the evening shadows deepened—her *Mamm* crying of grief and Lydia weeping as earnestly into her *Daed's* shoulder. To cause her *Eldre* this kind of pain seemed the worst she could do. Her, the *gut Dochder*.

After a while, Joel said, "Come. Come, Miriam. Come, Lydia. This does no one *gut*. Let us have supper. Time enough later to decide how to deal with this. I will go feed the chickens. It is probably well that Daniel is having supper with his *Eldre*. This way we do not need to worry about having long faces."

Their meal was eaten in silence. Lydia reflected, not for the first time, that those insane moments' comfort with Brock hadn't nearly been worth this depth of regret and sadness. If only she'd thought more—or at all—in her loneliness. She hated bringing this grief into her *Eldre's* lives. Even if she was flooded with love every time she remembered the little *Boppli* now growing inside her.

After most of the evening meal was consumed, her *Mamm* broke the pensive silence, saying in a strong voice. "There is only one thing to be done, if you won't marry Peter."

Both Lydia and Joel looked at her.

"Lydia must go to my Cousin Rachel's. She can have the *Boppli* there."

"But wouldn't she," Lydia's *Daed* said diffidently, "be more comfortable here...in her own home, my *Frau*? After all, this would be her first—"

"And after she has...given birth..., my cousin will be glad to keep the child there as her own." Miriam looked between them, saying with both determination and a shade of defiance on her face.

"Keep the child?" Joel echoed, surprise in his voice.

"If she marries, Lydia can, of course, keep the *Boppli*." Miriam shrugged. "It seems to be Peter Stromeyer or this."

"Give away my *Boppli*?" Dismay rippled through Lydia. "And I won't marry that old *Mann*!"

"Then, *yah*. Go to Rachel's and leave the *Boppli* to be raised by Rachel and her husband," Miriam said, seeming to waver before her voice strengthened again. She sounded almost cold now. "Both are *gut* people. It would be best for the *Boppli* to be raised by a *Mamm* and *Daed* and not to be here in Elizabethtown. Not to have any shadow of...this hovering over him or her. If you will not consider marrying. Remember, *Dochder*, there are consequences to our choices. You made your bed."

Shock held Lydia's voice suspended for a moment. After a moment, she said in a strangled voice, "I—I have spent many hours regretting—all this. My actions, the coming of this *Boppli*. So much. I—I was alone there on *rumspringa*. And lonely. I'd waited to take my *rumspringa*. Then, when I was there...I slipped...."

She bent her head over her plate, tears leaking down her cheeks in a salty trail and ended up dripping off her chin. "But...I cannot—I cannot marry Peter Stromeyer."

"I have to admit," feeling her heart churn inside her, she took a deep, shuddering breath, "I have to admit that I love this *Boppli*, *Mamm*. I cannot give it away."

"Of course, you do." Miriam reached her hand across the table to place it over Lydia's. "It is the way of *Eldre* to love their children. This is why I urge you to marry, even if Peter isn't the *Mann* you'd choose in other circumstances."

With a smile of gratitude at her *Mamm's* understanding, Lydia shifted her hand to squeeze Miriam's.

"Part of that love for your child," her *Mamm* continued, "is to do what is best for the *Boppli*. I'm sure all your *Geschwischder* would agree about this. If you will not marry, you must leave the *Boppli* with my cousin. Rachel only has the five children. It has been several years since her last and she's not likely to have more. Your *Boppli* can fit in there with no problem. I'm sure Rachel would do this for us. When we last spoke, she talked of wishing they could have more children."

Lydia's heart sank with her. She shuddered at the thought of marrying an old, sick *Mann*, but she felt ripped apart to think of giving birth and driving away without her child.

"It is that, my *Dochder*, or we can let it be known that you...that you were forced by this *Englischer*."

She looked up at her *Mamm*. "But...that wouldn't be true. He did not force me. This was a...a sinful choice of my own. I cannot accuse Brock of rape."

"Either way, whether you owned the sin before all our friends or accused this *Englischer* of forcing you, it would not be best for the *Boppli*." Her *Mamm's* mouth was set in a line. "Better to marry old Peter...or give the *Boppli* to Rachel and her *Mann*."

The next day, Daniel left the buggy shop, walking back to the back pasture through the thigh-high weeds and grass. He needed to find the time to tend the patch of grass since he was often out here to the storage or to fetch a buggy chassis. Joel and he had just finished the buggy ordered by Mercy and her new husband.

Daniel had to admit that, even though he no longer pined for Mercy—and probably hadn't ever really, given that he was to marry the woman—he was still a little relieved to have sent them off. They'd loaded into the new buggy after transferring a few things from Isaac's *Bruder's* buggy and left, leaving behind Kate's young relative for a visit here with Mercy's *Eldre*.

The sound of someone retching cut through Daniel's thoughts and brought him up short.

When he rounded the storage shed corner, he found Lydia there, looking pale as she straightened from where she'd kneeled next to the building. A streak of concern went through him and, at that moment, their gazes met.

"Sick again, Lydia?" He came up to stand beside her. "Am I to call your *Mamm* this time?"

"*Neh.*" She put up her hand to her black *kapp*, a strained smile on her face. "There is no need."

He felt his mouth pull down. "How can you say this? You are clearly not well. You should rest on your bed."

"Daniel," she seemed to draw herself up, bracing herself as she spoke, "have you no suspicion of what ails me?"

At her question, thoughts started revolving in his head. "Clearly, your stomach is upset."

To his dismay, Lydia gulped back what sounded like a sob, turning her face away. It seemed strange to see merry Lydia this way.

"I—I have sinned, Daniel. It must be obvious. It will soon be known to all." Her anguished words came out with a sob.

All the pieces of the puzzle came together with a snap then and realization as to what she meant hit him like a board between the eyes. Without thinking, he took a step toward her with his hand outstretched and then reminded himself that this was not the time to offer a comforting hug. Certainly not to a *Maedel* in Lydia's kind of distress.

Offering a hug was completely unlike him anyway and Daniel had no idea why he'd now felt the urge.

When she turned and gave him a brave smile, her usually-smiling brown eyes wet from her tears, he realized he felt shaken.

She gulped again, knuckling away the moisture at her cheek. "There is no good in regret, *yah*? Only—only I am gripped with it, but that is no reason to worry you. Just forget I spoke to you about it. I—I will find a way."

"Who is the father then? The *Mann* with whom you courted who left you in this situation?" Daniel ignored this, knowing his words came out with undue violence. He sounded angry, he recognized as he spoke. He drew in a breath to calm himself. The last thing Lydia needed was to deal with anger from him.

"Your *Daed*— Joel must know who to bring to justice. I will help him and the church elders do this." Daniel forced an apologetic smile. She didn't need him yelling at her. "Having returned to this area recently, I do not know with whom you've been courting... Who has over-stepped the bounds of decency."

Lydia shifted to walk back around the shed and he followed. She threw him another glance of guilt and regret. "It was me. I was the one who was indecent. You haven't been here and cannot know that I've not been courting with anyone."

Walking beside her through the crackling high grass, he threw her a startled look. "You haven't?"

"There were several *Menner* who wanted to court with me.... And old Peter Stromeyer actually asked me to court. He just wants a caretaker, though. My *Mamm* now says I should have done this." The mournful admission slipped from her as she batted aside several tall stalks of grass.

Daniel could keep the shock from his face. "That old *Mann*? Of course you wouldn't want to marry him, but was there no other? No young *Mann* courting with you?"

"*Neh*. No one. There was just no one who interested me. I—I ended up taking a delayed *rumspringa*." As they crossed the overgrown area, she again dropped her head, saying in a voice that sounded suffocated. "It happened then."

"That was when...?" He paused, the frown descending on to his face again. This all had to be so hard for her. It was odd to see cheerful Lydia this burdened.

She stopped at the fence gate next to the yard. "*Yah*, I did. I went not to stay with relatives or friends. I went to a town where I knew no one."

Holding the gate as he passed through, she said, "I went to Bedford."

Daniel felt his frown deepen. "East ways of here?"

"*Yah*." Despite the positive answer, she shook her *kapped* head, as if admonishing herself. "I took a job in a restaurant there that served travelers. Amish and *Englisch* alike."

"In the *Englischer* world?"

"Of course. Is that not what *rumspringa* is for? To make sure that we are making a clear choice when we join the church?"

He hated the sadness in her voice. It echoed in his head like his own. "It was there that you met...?"

"I met an *Englischer* named Brock." She swung to look at Daniel again. "He was going off to school a few weeks later to study to be a doctor. He'd already been accepted into the school. I understand that's a big thing. Anyway...it just happened."

"And he left you here." Daniel stopped her with his hand on her arm, his voice harsh and as stormy, echoing the riot in his chest. "He just left you here to deal with this."

Lydia shook her head. "He knows nothing of it. Here is where I want to be, Daniel. Like you. I do not want to live in the *Englischer* world with Brock or any other *Englischer*. I—I think that may have been why I was...different with him, instead of other *Englischers*. Less guarded. I knew he was leaving for training."

"Maybe that's why...why Brock seemed safe." Her admission was made in a low voice as she turned to cross the yard behind the *Haus*.

Following her, Daniel snagged her arm to hold her from moving forward. "What will you do, Lydia? You cannot marry Peter Stromeyer!"

She stopped, her set, pale face looking back at him. "I don't know yet what I will do. I created this. The...situation is of my own making. And now...now since I am refusing to tell Peter I will marry him, my *Mamm* wants me to go live with her cousin to have the *Boppli*...and leave it there to be raised by them. I—I don't know if I can do that."

He felt his brows draw together in another troubled frown. "Then what? You will stay here with your *Eldre* and hope...no one treats you and the *Boppli* badly? Differently?"

She smiled up at him, her beautiful brown eyes shadows. "I don't know what will happen, but I will have to deal with it somehow."

As the evening shadows fell that night, Daniel continued thinking about everything that had been discussed between him and Lydia. Every time he remembered the shift in her voice when she spoke of the *Boppli*—even though the child's existence was a constant reminder of her sin and even though her pregnancy was tearing her world apart—he felt a pit of something warm and squishy in his stomach. She loved her child.

As fall was settling into the countryside, it had grown chillier in Daniel's small room off the buggy shop. He carried a quilt over his shoulders as he got ready for bed, wondering at one point if it was of Lydia's making. He found himself staring at the fabric closely, noting that the small stitches there resembled the neat ones in the shirts she'd made for him.

Her situation kept revolving in his head and as Daniel sat in the plain, serviceable chair beside his bed, pulling off his shoes, he stopped, a thought striking him. The shoe in his hand dropped heedlessly to the floor. He didn't know why it hadn't occurred to him before.

Not old Peter Stromeyer, but maybe...

Lydia needed a *Mann*. Being married would mean that no one would comment about her coming child. It wouldn't even be mentioned in whispers as they didn't talk of such things. Of course, he probably hadn't thought of this before because she'd been so adamant that she was courting with no one.

And Daniel had been so revolted by the idea of her becoming that old *Mann's Frau*.

Still getting ready to climb into his narrow bed, he continued mulling over the problem, thinking of the various *Menner* that lived in their community. Maybe she'd overlooked someone, some other *Mann* besides old Peter.

Some were obviously—although this also was never openly discussed—courting with other *Maedels*. The trouble was that although there were several other unattached *Menner* in Elizabethtown, these were generally like the Abel Schrock, who worked in the buggy shop—*youngies* not ready to settle down. There really was no other unwed *Mann* here to marry her. In other circumstances, she'd probably have had to visit other Amish settlements to find a husband.

If not for this.

There was only…only himself.

He could marry Lydia. Be a *Daed* to her child and a husband to her.

The recognition sent a bolt through him. For the first time in a long while, he felt…he could actually benefit someone. And he liked Lydia. Having seen more of her since he worked for Joel, he'd come to like her even more. It also didn't hurt that she was a very good-looking girl, although the inside of a person was more important. She seemed…kind.

This almost made her…too *gut* for the likes of him.

Although Daniel had immediately felt the urge to himself suggest marriage to Lydia—her grief over potentially giving up her child had wrung his heart—he knew he didn't have much to offer. He was damaged, both battered by his own roiling grief and tainted in the eyes of the community. He needed to speak to Bishop Fisher about this.

Besides his name, Daniel had little to offer Lydia. He had no farm, no place to which to bring a *Frau*.

So powerfully did her dilemma sit on his mind that Daniel couldn't sleep, even after a hard day's labor. He blew out the single candle beside his bed and tucked himself securely into the blankets to keep out the seeping chill. Then, he lie in the dark, staring up at the ceiling, thinking about Lydia's warm brown eyes and brave smile. Thinking about how he'd be with a *Boppli* of his own.

He envisioned throwing a child in the air, sitting up with it at night when it was ill. Holding a small hand as he led his child to work with him.

He wanted to be a parent, to have *Kinder* of his own.

Slowly over the hours, he began to wonder if he wasn't the only real answer to Lydia's looming problem. The pitiful best. He needed to talk to the bishop.

Closing his eyes in the dark, Daniel began to pray.

Dear Gott, if this is something I should offer, tell me. Would she be worse off with my broken, even-more-sinful self? Should I speak and let her decide?

As slumber began to pull at him, he still had no answer from *Gott*, but he knew he wasn't forgotten. It would become clear.

The next morning before breakfast, Daniel tugged at Lydia's apron string, hissing for her to come outside on the porch.

Startled, Lydia looked up from the steaming plate of food she'd started to carry to the table. "What? Now?"

"*Yah.* Now"

His voice was gruff, even for Daniel, and he seemed so serious, she settled the plates on the table quickly and followed him out to porch on the back of the *Haus*.

"Lydia," he said abruptly, seeming to frown angrily down at the boards beneath their feet. "You and I have grown up together. You know…everything about me."

"*Yah.* I know you," she said, not sure what this was all about.

He drew a breath before capturing her hand and urging her over to a ladder-back chair that sat on the porch. "Here. Sit. I have something I-I need to make sure you understand. Before I say anything else, you must hear this."

She sat down in the chair he moved her toward, startled by his odd manner. "Of course. You can tell me whatever you need to, Daniel."

"It is not that—" He looked up at her, meeting her gaze. "You deserve to know everything before—before I go on."

"Ooookay."

Taking in another long breath, he sat down in the chair next to her. "I woke early and went to talk to Bishop Fisher about this. Despite his encouragement for me to offer myself, I—I feel I must make sure you know all about me."

Distressed by his obvious distress, she reached a hand out to him.

"Lydia, I have been a fool. A faithless, *Gott*-less fool." Daniel looked up. "You know that Mercy and I courted—and planned to marry."

"*Yah.*" This wasn't news to Lydia and it puzzled her to have him speak of it now as an admission.

"I left her—almost at the altar. When I went away from here for my *rumspringa*, I-I was afraid of the *Englischer* world. I ran from my own *rumspringa* there to my *Onkle's Haus.*"

He seemed to fight for words. "I was…afraid. Afraid that I couldn't make it in the *Englischer* world on my own, without my *Daed* and my friends. I am almost the youngest in my *familye*. I only have one younger sister."

"*Yah.* Rebecca."

"I have—I guess I have been babied some." He shook his head. "It isn't important. I have no excuse for deserting Mercy and leaving the church—leaving our world. I thought I needed to go back, to make myself face my fears. I left this life."

Lydia dropped her gaze to the porch boards now. "I remember. The church members…voted to shun you."

"*Yah*. To protect all the others." He hung his head. "Even my *Eldre* wouldn't speak to me."

After a moment, Daniel straightened to look at her. "You know I have repented and come back to the church. Bishop Fisher has—has helped in many ways. It was through him and the other bishops that your *Daed* was encouraged to give me this job after I returned."

"My father gave you a job when your own *Eldre* didn't welcome you back, even giving their farm to your *Schweschder's* husband," she said tartly. "Even though you'd repented before all and been accepted back as a member in the church."

He looked at her sadly. "This is why I bring up my past, Lydia. There are those here who were hurt by my foolish actions. Those who don't trust me any longer. My *Eldre* were hurt…and it's understandable that they believe Judith's *Mann* is more…deserving."

Not knowing why he brought up all this with her, she waited with a wrinkled brow.

Daniel's gaze was steady. "I want you to know that I don't have much. I have a wicked, wrongful past, worse than most, but if you—you would accept me, I will be faithful all my life."

"Accept you?" Stunned and unsure of his meaning, Lydia stared back at him.

He didn't again reach for her hand now, his dangling between his knees as he sat in the chair next to hers on the porch.

"*Yah*. You cannot accept old Peter Stromeyer, but… But maybe I can help. Will you marry me, Lydia? As I said, I will be faithful to you and to *Gott* all my life. I will try to be the best husband I can be…and I want to be a *Daed* to your child. If you think this would be *gut*."

She felt as if her breath were suspended in her chest. "You…you want to marry me?"

"*Yah*, if you will align yourself with a *Mann* as broken as me." He looked at her steadily. "I want to have *Kinder* with you. Be everything a *Mann* is supposed to be. Live in *Gott's* hand."

"But, Daniel," her heart thundered within her chest. "you...know what I did. That I bring with me a *Boppli*."

"I do." He reached out to capture the hand she'd gestured with. "I do know this and I want to raise this *Boppli* with you ...as our own child."

So stunned by his unexpected proposal, she stared blindly at yard behind the *Haus*.

Marry Daniel?

He...this seemed as if he were offering her everything she needed to raise her child herself. But she'd leapt blindly before...that was what got her into this situation and what had already threatened the little *Boppli* she carried inside her.

"Let me think, Daniel." She stretched out a hand towards him. "I must think."

"*Yah*. You must certainly think. That is why I reminded you about myself." He sent her a smile of understanding. "You must certainly think."

CHAPTER FOUR

The kitchen at the Schrock *Haus* was busy with chattering women after the church meeting. It was two days after Daniel's surprising proposal and Lydia still didn't know how to answer him.

She definitely needed a husband. Marrying old Peter Stromeyer was not to even be considered, but Daniel... She'd been so wrong in her actions before. All the prayers she'd uttered since his proposal hadn't brought this any clearer yet.

"Over here, Anna." Lydia smiled as she dragged her thoughts back to the present, positioning Kate Miller's young cousin next to her to peel more potatoes.

"*Denki*," Anna said gratefully, coming to work next to Lydia. Kate and her husband, Enoch, had gone back to Mannheim, leaving the young woman there to "widen her acquaintance."

Everyone knew that phrase indicated that Anna Lehmann was of an age to marry and looking around for a *gut Mann*. Lydia just didn't know who the girl would find in Elizabethtown. Maybe she and one of the younger *Menner* would connect.

"Excuse me." Hagar Hershberger slipped past the sink, juggling two loaded platters in her hands with a grin on her face.

"There are certainly a lot of dishes to do," Anna commented with a smile, plunging her hands in the soapy water.

"Always," Lydia agreed.

"Hello!" Amity Schrock—younger sister to the Abel Schrock that worked in the buggy shop alongside her *Daed* and Daniel—appeared at the sink. "Your sister, Naomi sent me over, Lydia. She said you've been here washing dishes a while and need to come eat with her."

Smiling her gratitude at the *Maedel*, Lydia said as she reached for a towel to dry her hands, "*Denki*, Amity."

She nodded toward Anna. "Amity, meet Anna Lehmann. She's visiting here from Mannheim and has also volunteered for dish washing duty. You, two, are about the same age. You should meet."

"Go ahead," Anna said to Lydia with a shy smile. "Eat with your sister."

"I think I will." Lydia nodded as she left the girls at the sink, heading to get herself a plate of food. Although she'd never admit it, she'd started feeling unaccountably tired lately.

Weaving her way through the last of the diners, she made her way to where her sister sat alone under a tree.

"It's about time you finished helping in there," Naomi greeted her.

"Thank you, *Schweschder*." Lydia sank down to the ground beside her. Of all her siblings, she felt closest to Naomi whom she'd always looked after. Yes, her sister could be self-centered, but that was often a result of being the youngest child.

"We haven't had a chance to talk alone." Her sister leaned a little closer, as if the others milling around the yard could overhear her. "Did you tell *Mamm* and *Daed*?"

"*Yah*," Lydia said heavily. "It was the hardest thing I've ever done."

Just the remembrance of her *Mamm's* tears and the fact that she often looked sad now made Lydia cringe. For several seconds, she'd even considered her *Mamm's* suggestion that she marry old Peter.

"I can imagine." Naomi shifted, tucking her skirt more firmly under her. "What did they say? Did they have any idea what you should do?"

"They did," swallowing, Lydia said, "but that's not the biggest thing we have to talk about. *Mamm* has said what she thinks is best—since I won't even consider marrying Peter Stromeyer—but I've also had a different marriage proposal."

Naomi slewed around to stare at her more fully. "You have? Really? From who? You aren't courting with anyone and does this *Mann* know that—"

"*Yah.*" Lydia interrupted, flushing with annoyance. "Do you think I would marry a *Mann* without telling him?"

"You're—you're going to marry?" Naomi's eyes seemed to bug out. "Who is this? Who would propose? And why not consider Peter Stromeyer.... I mean, he is old..."

"*Yah,*" Lydia shot back, "older than *Daed* and sick, too."

"Well, if not him, then who? Who else is there to even propose?"

"It is Daniel Stoltzfus." Lydia looked up to meet her sister's gaze. "You know the *Mann* who works now with *Daed?*"

Her *Schweschder* leaned closer, hissing with a pointed stare, "Of course, I know who Daniel Stoltzfus is! He was only a grade or two ahead of me in school. Besides, everyone knows who he is. He's the *Mann* we voted in church to shun last year. It caused more talk than I can ever remember."

Lydia kept a steady gaze on Naomi. "*Yah.* And then Daniel returned, made his confession to the church elders and members to rejoin. And now—now he has asked me to marry him."

"Oh." Her sister stared at her a moment without saying anything, then reached over to grasp Lydia's hand. "Okay. What do *Mamm* and *Daed* say you should do? Do they know Daniel Stoltzfus asked you to marry him, even with his past?"

She grasped her sister's hand. "*Neh.* They don't know. And I've not yet agreed to wed Daniel. Naomi, I know he—he now represents a risk. I remember everything Mercy went through."

Naomi's gaze sharpened on her as her eyebrows lowered. "Daniel Stoltzfus wants to raise your child as his own?"

A glow of happiness glimmered in Lydia's chest to hear the possibility spoken aloud. "*Yah.* That was what he said."

"As if the *Boppli* were his own? And...and you will never even tell the *Englischer* that he has a child?"

Hearing an odd note in her sister's voice, Lydia said, "I don't think telling Brock about this *Boppli* would be best for anyone."

Still clasping Lydia's hand, her sister said, "Possibly not. Still…if I were a *Mann*, I'd want to know."

"Most *Menner* don't think of this as we do," Lydia said, feeling unaccountably defensive although she knew Naomi wasn't criticizing her in this.

"And you think you will accept Daniel's proposal, even though you know about him. That he is a risk? What if he leaves the church again? Runs off to the *Englischer* world again and leaves you high and dry, like he did Mercy?"

Tightening her grasp on Naomi's fingers, Lydia swallowed. "At least… If he does that, at least I would have given this child a name and I could raise it as my own. Is it not the same with Peter Stromeyer? He is ancient and will not be able to raise a *Boppli*. I will not marry him. *Schweschder, Mamm* has suggested I go to stay with her cousin, Rachel, to have the *Boppli*…and leave it there with Cousin Rachel to raise. As her own child."

Naomi tilted her head, sympathy slipping onto her face. "Oh, Lydia."

"You know," Lydia tried on a wavering smile. "You know, I've always talked of being a *Mamm*. Looked forward to the day when I will have a *Boppli* of my own. I cannot give away my child."

Her sister nodded, tears suddenly swimming in her eyes. "*Yah*, I do know this about you, but you said it yourself, this Daniel is a risk! What good is it to marry a *Mann* who may…leave you? I understand you not marrying old Peter, but still… Is this better than giving the *Englischer's* child to *Mamm's* cousin?"

"I don't know. I know Daniel could leave again, given his past." Her gaze leveling as she stared past her sister, she repeated, "I know, but the *Boppli* is my child, Naomi. I'm—I'm still trying to decide what is best."

She sent up a silent prayer to *Gott* to help her with this.

The next morning, Daniel swung the scythe, cutting the tall weeds in a swipe of the blade. A cool wind ruffled the long grass in the field near the storage shed. He had no idea what Lydia planned to do, but ever since he'd spoken to Bishop Fisher, prayed to *Gott* and offered to marry her to be a *Daed* to her *Boppli*, he'd felt at peace.

An image of Lydia's smiling brown eyes rose up before him. Through her, he could have *Kinder* of his own. Children to whom he could be a *gut*, loving *Daed*.

Marrying a comely woman like Lydia wouldn't be a hardship, either.

He'd done some stupid, senseless things in the past year, but the thought of marrying and being a father to her children settled smoothly into his ruffled soul. Thinking about it—even with his income compromised by no longer having a farm of his own—made him the happiest he'd been in a long time.

Feeling a smile grow on his face at the memory of Lydia's surprise at his proposal, he mopped his forehead, put his hat back on his and went back to scything. The woman drew him and might have even if she hadn't come with a ready-made family.

Feeling the stretch in his muscles as he swung the blade to cut short the tall, brown grass, he drew in a breath of autumn coolness. As he worked, the distant hum of some *Englischer's* plow working in a distant field could be heard. Daniel had no doubts as to the wisdom of his returning to this life, even if Lydia didn't decide in his favor, although he hoped with all himself that she did.

He'd been such a foolish, doubting *lappich Buwe* before, forgetting that *Gott* loved him even in all his stupidity. He had only to align himself with his Creator to draw on this love. It still stung Daniel to think that he'd so forgotten this that he'd thrown aside his whole life.

Hearing steps behind him in the crispy, newly-shorn fall growth, he turned to see Lydia crossing the field, passing a row of the extra buggy bodies stored there.

"*Goedemorgen*, Lydia." He leaned on the scythe handle, removing his broad-brimmed hat to wipe his sleeve across his sweaty forehead again.

"*Goedemorgen*." She stopped three or four feet away. "I have...questions for you, Daniel Stoltzfus. Can we talk?"

"Of course," he invited, slipping back on his hat. "Ask me whatever. I will answer anything you like."

Her face seemed troubled. "You know I am expecting a child."

"*Yah*." He knew this would trouble most *Menner*.

"And that the father of this child is an *Englischer*." She swallowed.

Daniel shifted his arm on the scythe's long handle. "If you marry me, Lydia, I will be the *Boppli's Daed*. Me. It will be my child, carry my name and live in our *Haus*. I will teach it right from wrong, always listening to the *Boppli's* questions, always caring for this child. It will never know of any other father, this I promise."

The troubled look still on her face she said, "*Yah*...but will you ever be able to love this...this bastard child?"

Letting the scythe fall to the ground, he moved to her and took her hand. "With all my heart, Lydia. I promise you this. The *Boppli* will be ours. Yours and mine, not an *Englischer's* bastard. Our child. No word otherwise will ever cross my lips and the child will never know another *Mann* as a father. Please do not think I will favor our other children over this, our first. I know you've spoken to Bishop Fisher about this, but if we marry and raise the child as our own, he will not speak of it to any other person."

Lydia's *kapp*-covered head tilted back as she stared into his face.

"My child. No one else is to be told differently. No one else need know." He looked into her brown eyes. "If you marry me, this little *Boppli* will be my child."

There was frost on the grass tips the next morning as Daniel walked across the drive from the buggy shop. He blew on his fingers, looking forward to Lydia's coffee. She had a knack of brewing it that seemed to wake up his mornings even more.

Just as his foot was on the first step, he spotted a small solitary figure trudging up the drive to Joel Troyer's home.

Standing with his hands tucked in his armpits for warmth, Daniel watched the boy.

"Mark!" he called out as the slight figure drew nearer. "What's going on? Did your *Grossdaddi* send you for another buggy reflector?"

"*Neh*," the boy answered in a sullen voice as he drew nearer.

"Then what can we do to help you?" Daniel was gentle in his inquiry. Something about this glowering boy reminded him of himself, although he'd never been as…as free to be visible with his displeasure when he was younger. Maybe he should have been.

He'd always been—always required himself to be, as did his *Daed*—acceptable to others. He handled things himself and did not upset anyone else.

Clearly, Mark wasn't concerned about this.

"I have to ask if you need help here." Mark's surly words were almost inaudible.

"Here?" Daniel bit back a smile. He'd seldom seen a more hostile request for a job. "In the buggy shop?"

"*Yah*." The *scholar* shot him a smoldering upwards glance. "My *Grossdaddi* said."

Shifting around to lean on the porch handrail, Daniel let his gaze rest on the youth. "You know, Mark, you don't seem like a *Buwe* who is craving to find work."

The scowl on the youth's face deepened. "I'm not, but *Grossdaddi* made— Well, I'm here to ask."

Even if Daniel hadn't owed his re-admittance to this life to Bishop Fisher and the other church leaders listening to *Gott* and deciding in his favor, he still would have felt compassionate towards Mark.

He sat down on the steps, bringing him to the boy's level. "Why would your *Grossdaddi* do that? Send you here?"

"I don't know. At least I don't have to go to that stinky school with my *Bruders!*" The words burst angrily out of Mark. "Do you need help or not?"

Shoving up a finger to tilt his broad-brimmed hat back on his head, Daniel said, "I don't know. We can ask Joel. It's his shop."

Mark looked at him, anger smoldering on his sullen features.

Daniel rose to his feet, his hand on Mark's thin shoulder. "Come on in. It's warmer inside. We'll ask him if he has a job for you."

Leaving the boy to follow him up the steps, Daniel headed toward the back door of the *Haus.*

"I know about you!" Mark looked up at him from the bottom of the steps, a triumphant accusation mixing with the glowering expression on his face. "You left the church for the *Englischer* world. You were even shunned!"

His hand on the porch rail, Daniel paused to look at Mark. The boy said nothing, but the truth and Daniel had faced worse. It was only natural that many in the community doubted him now.

"*Yah.* I did," he admitted without hesitation, "…and I was shunned. Before I returned and repented."

Seeming thrown by the easy admission, Mark's sullen expression deepened as he ducked his head. "I don't see why you were shunned. It's not as if you killed anyone."

Daniel turned to settle back on the upper step. He looked into the boy's rebellious, angry face. "*Neh*, I didn't commit that sin, but I disappointed and hurt many."

"How? You just left!" The words burst out of Mark as he glowered at Daniel.

Not sure what all was going on inside Bishop Fisher's grandson's head, Daniel just nodded. "This isn't an easy life, Mark. The shunning was to protect the others here. I wasn't…wasn't very kind or…safe to them or myself."

"I don't know why you came back," Mark muttered, stomping up the steps past Daniel.

Later that day when Daniel was wrestling a recalcitrant wheel back onto a buggy in the shop and the shop was empty, Lydia stepped into the buggy shop, pausing next to Daniel's work area. Other than the boy her *Daed* had hired who was sweeping out his inner office, she and Daniel were alone.

She knew she didn't have long to make a decision. Just that morning, her *Mamm* had spoken again about Lydia going to stay with Cousin Rachel, since she wouldn't consider approaching old Peter about marriage.

Looking up from the wheel, Daniel smiled at her. "*Goedenmorgan*, Lydia. I missed you at breakfast."

"*Yah*, I wasn't hungry this morning." In truth, her stomach had been in such revolt, she'd stayed in bed.

She now leaned back against the buggy he on which he worked, her chin lifting as she looked his way, a smile played on her lips. "Daniel Stoltzfus, you are a puzzle…and a risk. You know that, don't you?"

He glanced back at the wheel, his mouth quirking in response. "Why would you say that, Lydia Troyer, when I'm an open book to you?"

Walking over to perch on a backless stool near the rear of the buggy, she ignored his question as if he hadn't spoken. "You cannot be unaware that you are a—a black sheep to most. A heartbreaker. Others haven't forgotten how you treated Mercy, even if she did go on to marry another."

"And they shouldn't forget my actions." Daniel leaned his shoulder against it to snug the wheel on more fully. "I was wrong to have let things go as they did with Mercy."

Her hands tucked under the sides of her skirt where she perched on the stool, Lydia said, "You were wrong not to marry her, even though you ran off?"

Looking the buggy over with an accustomed eye, she then glanced his way. Since even before he'd proposed and offered her a way to keep her *Boppli*, she'd not be able to keep from noticing Daniel. The easy stance of his lean figure and his broad hands made her insides warm up in a way she didn't think they should.

Daniel shot her a look. "*Neh*, I wasn't wrong not to marry her. I was wrong to have planned marriage with anyone since I was so unsettled myself."

"And you're more settled now?" She looked at him, hope and doubt battling inside her. Her prayers had grown more desperate through these few days and she wondered now how she could help but accept him. The thought of marrying old Peter Stromeyer made her shudder and she couldn't consider giving her *Boppli* to someone else.

She hesitated to accept Daniel's proposal, but it felt right to marry him…and there seemed no better answer. Lydia couldn't help, but feel *Gott* was giving her a response to her prayers in the form of this damaged *Mann*.

"*Yah*." Fitting on the buggy wheel nuts, Daniel looked up. "I believe I am more settled. I aim to follow *Gott's* laws. I repent daily."

"And you are not a risk?" She asked, her gaze fixed on the buggy wheel before glancing at him.

Daniel didn't answer immediately, pausing to stare at her as he reached over to scratch gently at his bicep. "Lydia, I know I'm an unsure choice for any woman."

He went back to screwing on the buggy wheel nuts before looking up at her again. "But I have faced darkness…and have come back to the light. I believe I have learned."

Drawn to him and torn at the same time, Lydia thought of her sister's words and looked at him silently.

"Of course," he smiled over at her, "there will always be more for us to learn while we are here on this earth."

"If you had a *Frau* and a *familye*, where would you live?"

Shaking his head, he responded, "I don't know where exactly—other than my room off the shop, but I will always care for my wife and children."

"Daniel," she said with sudden impulsivity, "do you really want to take on a *Frau* now…and one who brings with her someone else's *Boppli*?"

"Lydia," he straightened to his feet, coming over to stand in front of her stool. "As I have told you, when we marry, this will not be 'someone else's *Boppli*.' It will be ours. Yours and mine. And we will raise our son or daughter together, as we will do everything from that moment on. It will be our child. My *Boppli*. No one else's."

Feeling her eyes fill, she asked him in a strangled voice, "How can you be so sure of this? Of me? You and Mercy courted—"

He stopped her with a dismissive wave. "*Yah*, I know. I made poor choices with Mercy. But she and I were—were *youngies*. I was ignorant and foolish. My actions in the last year proved how foolish I was."

Daniel stood a foot in front of her, so close Lydia could imagine she felt the heat of his body despite the fact that it wasn't cold in the shop.

"How can I know that you and I belong together? I—I just do." His words came out with conviction.

Lydia found the words spilling out of her. "Then—then, *yah*. I will marry you, Daniel, if you're sure."

"I am. I am sure." A smile broadened over his face. "More sure of this than I have been of anything since my return. Let's marry. I will be your *Mann* and you my *Frau*."

CHAPTER FIVE

The next day, Lydia leaned back in a porch chair, rocking gently as a chilly fall breeze brushed against her heated cheeks.

Appearing suddenly at the porch rail between two short evergreen bushes, Daniel looked at her steadily. "You didn't come in to eat breakfast again."

She swallowed against the all-too-familiar rebellion in her midsection, stretching her mouth into a smile. "*Neh*. I'm not hungry."

"You must keep up your strength. Particularly now." He looked at her steadily, sympathy in his eyes.

"It is silly," she sucked in another steadying breath, "to call this 'morning sickness.' More like anytime sickness."

"I'm sorry." He rested bare forearms against the rail, wearing no jacket despite the cold air. "You can't go without eating, though. Not completely."

"*Neh*, of course, not." She gulped in another breath, leaning her head back.

"My eldest *Schweschder* had troubles like this," Daniel said. "She found that eating a little—keeping something on her stomach—helped settle it. You should try to eat something."

"I don't know…" She flexed her fingers on the arms of the porch chair, slowly shaking her head.

Daniel shook his head. "Just a minute."

Suddenly he dropped out of sight, disappearing from the porch rail, and Lydia leaned forward to look for him, bouncing back in her chair when he popped up again to face her.

"So, okay. If—if you will take a few bites of something, I have a gift for you."

"A gift?"

"*Yah*. Wait here." He went over to the porch stairs and came up to her level, his steps echoing on the deck as he bounded into the *Haus*.

The screen door banged shut behind him as he returned.

"Take a few bites of this." Daniel offered her a small hunk of bread.

"Did my *Mamm* give you that?" Lydia stared at the bread in surprise.

"*Yah*. Of course. She likes me." Daniel shrugged as if he had no idea how formidable her *Mamm* could be.

"Daniel…" She looked at the hunk of bread he held out to her. "I…don't think…"

"You just need to try it," he said in a coaxing tone she'd never thought to hear from such a manly *Mann*.

"Nibble on the bread—" he disappeared down the steps, crouching down again, "—and I'll give you these…as a reward. A bribe."

To her astonishment, he'd held up a fistful of purple asters. She remembered now that the purple star-like flowers had sprouted in huddled clumps at the base of the shrubs around the porch.

"Really?" She found herself laughing at his unexpected silliness. "You think this will tempt me? Flowers pulled from my yard?"

"*Yah*," he said with a crooked smile that sent a warm glow into her chest. "We will put them in water for you to look at. One of *Gott's* glories that has lingered despite the chilly weather. What better incentive when you're growing another of His glories inside you?"

Lydia smiled at his silliness. "Hand me the bread."

"Just nibble on it," he instructed, giving it to her along with the flowers he'd picked.

She felt tears spring to her eyes at the kindness in his voice. For so long now she hadn't felt she deserved forbearance from anyone and even though her *Daed* was kind, her *Mamm's* worry had made the older woman short-tempered.

"And don't skip eating this evening. You will need your strength for our talk with your *Eldre*." Daniel smiled at her before turning away.

Watching him jog across the drive to the buggy shop, Lydia swallowed, hoping she was doing the right thing. Daniel seemed so *gut* and kind, but was marrying him the best choice?

"What do you mean?" Miriam Troyer gasped later that evening.

Daniel reached out to grasp Lydia's hand, repeating, "I would like to marry your daughter."

Lydia sat like stone, aware of the unfamiliar pressure of his fingers. When couples courted, it was expected that they would exchange chaste kisses as well as hugs. Some Amish even had their courting *youngies* bundle together in the same bed with only a board between them. While this allowed no physical contact, the couple usually spent many evenings exchanging thoughts and hopes.

She and Daniel had done none of this…and the touch of his hand over hers brought the reality home to her. She was agreeing to marry this *Mann*, to spend her earthly life with him. To sleep in his bed. She was entrusting herself and her child into the hands of a *Mann* who had abandoned one woman already. What if she were wrong?

Again?

Even though she'd stupidly given into loneliness and Brock's entreaties that once, she still felt shy at the thought of sleeping beside Daniel. For a *Maedel* who was to have a child outside of wedlock, this was silly.

Lydia noted absently that a log in the fireplace hissed in the silence as her *Eldre* appeared to grope for words, the sound shooting through the gentle crackle of the fire that kept the room warm.

"Lydia and I have agreed to marry," Daniel repeated, glancing over at Joel, who was still silent. "I will make her a *gut* husband, Joel. You can rely on this."

"You know—? Lydia, have you told him...everything?" Her *Mamm* seemed angry, but Lydia knew this was her usual look when agitated.

"*Yah*. Everything." She steadily met her *Mamm's* glare. "He knows about...the *Boppli*... About the *Englischer*. Everything."

Miriam Troyer seemed to struggle to know what to say.

"And still, you want to marry my Lydia?" Joel spoke finally, his question calm. "Why?"

Daniel's gaze dropped to where his hands rested on the table top. Dinner had been eaten and the dirty plates stacked by the sink. The tablecloth was bare now, except for several serving pieces and a few crumbs on the cloth.

Looking up, Daniel responded to her *Daed*. "I do want to marry Lydia. I will be honest, Joel. I think Lydia is fine and I have need of a wife. I want very much to have a *familye*. I am ready to marry and settle down. I believe Lydia and I are well-suited. We like each other. We have spoken—she and I—and we are both committed to follow *Gott* in a plain, simple life and to raise the *Boppli* as our child. My child and hers. No other father will even be spoken of."

Watching her *Daed's* face, she saw Daniel turn toward her with another smile. "We hope *Gott* blesses us with a large *familye*."

"You have definitely decided not to go to Cousin Rachel's?" Miriam questioned her *Dochder*, as if still wrestling to comprehend this. "You—you will marry Daniel instead? You have not been courting, you two."

Sending her mother a reassuring smile, Lydia said, "No, I will not go to Cousin Rachel and I will not give my *Boppli* away. Daniel and I will marry. Not having a long courtship does not matter. I have known him my entire life, *Mamm*. We grew up in the same school."

"And since I came to work for Joel," Daniel reached out his hand to take Lydia's, "we have spent more time together."

"You have spoken to Bishop Fisher about the marriage?" Her *Daed* looked keenly at Daniel.

"About offering marriage, yes. Not since then, as I wanted to talk to you first, Joel." Daniel met his gaze steadily. "If you give us your approval, I will go to the bishop tomorrow…and marry Lydia as soon as permitted."

Miriam Troyer seemed to ignore this interchange, reaching out to clutch Lydia's arm. "Think carefully, my *Dochder*. You know I like Daniel fine, but if Rachel raises the child, you can return here to your life to court and marry…whoever. You will be clean of this—this mistake."

Lydia shook her head, placing a hand over her *Mamm's*. "No, I wouldn't be. I want—and my *Boppli* deserves this from me—to be a *Mamm* to this baby. Daniel and I, we—we will be fine. I like him, too."

Her *Daed's* chair scraped against the floor as he pushed it back to stand. "Since this is your wish, I give you my blessing, Daniel. *Gott* directs us all and I know He will be with you both."

A hiccupping sob escaped Miriam and she quickly stuffed a corner of her apron in her mouth.

Joel sent her what was for him a stern glance. "We both wish you well."

Relieved to have accomplished this hurdle, Lydia still felt a little sick to her stomach. She reminded herself, though, that this had pretty much been the case in the last few weeks. *Gott* directed them and promised His presence, but that didn't mean the road on this earth was always clear.

A day later, Daniel stood in the brisk morning air next to the black buggy parked in front of the buggy shop's wide door, smiling at his former fiancée. "Thank you so much, Mercy. Lydia...she has much need for this."

He nodded toward the small sack she'd given him.

"It's a good thing Isaac and I were passing back through Elizabethtown on our way to our next relative visit." A blonde curl escaping from her white *kapp*, his old friend grinned at him, huddling in her coat. "And it's good I happen to have an anti-nausea preparation with me in case of buggy sickness."

"*Denki* for stopping by. I'm glad your *Mamm* got my message to you...and *denki* for this cure." He cleared his voice awkwardly. "I have news."

Daniel shifted his hat in his hand, his smile spontaneously widening at the thought of the woman who would soon be his *Frau* and the mother of his *Bopplis*. "We are to marry, Lydia Troyer and I. Soon. And I'm not disappearing before this ceremony."

Having Joel's blessing meant a lot and it felt good to share the news.

"To marry? You and Lydia?" Mercy smiled, her face filled with surprise. "Congratulations!"

He nodded. It seemed fitting that Mercy would be the first to know, somehow. Of course, he'd expected that she would be glad for him. She was long over the bad time he'd put her through, jilting her before leaving for the *Englisch* world. She'd even insisted he not apologize for this again.

Mercy leaned in closer, her eyebrows lifted as she lowered her voice, her words making puffs in the cold air. "And you need—Lydia needs—something for nausea, even though she's not taking a buggy trip?"

She raised quizzical brows. "Maybe it's a *gut* thing you're marrying soon."

"*Yah.* I am very glad she's agreed to have me." He ducked his head a little, not able to keep from smiling.

With his subsequent upwards glance, he noted Mercy's grin peeping out from behind the laughing, scandalized look she sent his way and Daniel felt another wave of relief. There was no denying that although she seemed better than fine now, he still felt bad about the situation with Mercy. She did seem truly happy with Isaac, though, in a way she'd never seemed with Daniel.

"You must be glad for a soon marriage—and to be a *Daed*. You always looked forward to that." Mercy offered her hand to shake his as her Isaac climbed into the buggy beside her. "Well, the best to you both. Isaac and I must start off now!"

Stepping back, he waved as she and her husband drove their new buggy down the drive.

Returning to the inside of the shop where he'd been working with Abel—while Bishop Fisher's grandson, Mark, in a corner sullenly sorted nuts and bolts into their proper bins—Daniel stepped over to brace with one hand the unsteady undercarriage Abel was working on. His co-worker was crouched on the cement floor beneath one section.

"That was Mercy—what's her name now that she's a *Frau*?"

"Miller," Daniel responded in a laconic voice, reaching up to scratch his ear with the hand that still held the bag of anti-nausea herbs from Mercy.

"No regrets?" Abel gestured toward the drive where Mercy's buggy had sat before she and Isaac drove away.

Daniel huffed a short laugh. "Lots…but not about Mercy. Her Isaac seems like a *gut Mann* and she seems very happy with him. Very."

Abel wrestled with the buggy frame with several grunts of annoyance, finally diving fully under it. Daniel held his part firmly as the frame wiggled with Abel's exertions. After several pungent exclamations—including him yelling *dumm hund*! at the frame—the younger *Mann* emerged a few moments later. With a liberal smear of grease on one cheekbone and a triumphant gleam in his eyes, he announced with a victorious cackle, "There! Got it."

Chuckling at the sight of him, his hair standing on end, a broad smile on his face, Daniel just shook his head with a grin. "I'm glad the frame didn't drop on you. I must say, Abel, that working with you is always entertaining. I could never have had this much fun on a farm."

A wood stove hissed in the corner of the shop, heating the chilly space.

Daniel held the herbal cloth bag down to his side as he spoke to the other man. "I've got to go to the *Haus* a moment. I'll be right back."

"Okay." Abel headed back under the now-secure buggy frame.

With broad steps, Daniel mounted the back porch steps in the cold, rapping on the door. Hopefully, Lydia's *Mamm* didn't answer. This was for Lydia and he didn't feel like explaining it to her *Mamm*.

After a few moments, Lydia herself opened the door. "Daniel!"

Although he lived in the small room next to the shop, she seemed surprised to see him, glancing back over her shoulder.

He knew her *Mamm* wasn't exactly excited about their marriage, even though the woman seemed not to resent him personally in any way.

"*Yah.*" He thrust the bag toward her. "Mercy said to make a tea of this to—to calm your stomach. I'll see you at dinner."

The cloth bag in her hands as she stepped forward, closing the door behind her to keep out the chill, Lydia stared at him.

She took a deep breath before asking quietly, "Are you still sure, Daniel? You don't have to do this. No one would expect you to raise another *Mann's* child."

Already turned to jog back down the steps, he reached back, stretching out his hand to cover hers, still clutching the bag. "I'm sure. And this isn't another *Mann's* child, Lydia, but mine."

Before the service started the following Sunday, Naomi exclaimed, "You are not going to marry him!? Daniel Stoltzfus?"

After taking some of the tea Daniel had gotten from Mercy, Lydia's stomach felt better this morning than it had in days.

"Lower your voice!" Lydia hissed at her, glancing around to see if her sister's unguarded utterance had attracted attention. The heated room was still filling with church members who chattered as they found seats.

In a lower decibel, but with as much emphasis, Naomi asked again, "And *Daed* and *Mamm* approve of this? You have definitely decided on it, have you? Perhaps you should consider again. I have been thinking, Lydia—"

Putting her hand on her *Schweschder's* knee and gently squeezing it through her thick skirt when Naomi's voice started getting louder again, Lydia commented in a low volume, "Perhaps you and I should talk about this later. It's settled. Yes, *Daed* and *Mamm* approve."

"We shouldn't talk later," Naomi muttered. "And whether or not you and Daniel have told our *Eldre*, this might not be what you need to do. I have been thinking that it might not be so bad for you to go to Cousin Rachel."

Lydia swiveled toward her, "No! It is settled. You know if I don't marry, *Mamm* means me to—"

"I know—leave the *Boppli*—" Naomi finished in a low voice. "But maybe that wouldn't be so terrible! You could always visit there. It's not that far away and I'm sure Cousin Rachel would be glad to have you."

Flushed and trembling, Lydia opened her mouth to protest.

"And you cannot deny that Rachel and her *Mann* are happy together," Naomi inserted. "They would give the *Boppli* a good home. They have a pleasant *familye* and nice *Kinder*. Isn't it better for the *Boppli* to be raised there? Better than being raised by a *Mann* who has rejected his faith—even if he later repented and returned to this life. Who knows if he'll continue to walk in *Gott's* way?"

Oddly enough, Lydia felt as defensive for Daniel as she was revolted by the thought of allowing anyone else to raise her child. "No, *Schweschder*, giving the *Boppli* to Rachel would not be better. *Daed* agrees with my marrying Daniel. He actually seems glad about it. And you are not giving Daniel enough credit. He and I can create a pleasant *familye* together. He made a terrible mistake and he's paying the price for that, but *Gott* still loves him. Daniel has repented and re-entered the church. He's learned hard lessons. Why can we not forgive him if *Gott* has? *Daed* and *Mamm* have, as have I. Daniel is now accepted at our services and is no longer shunned."

"And you know for sure that he will never again do the same thing?" Naomi questioned in a waspish tone.

"Have we not been directed to forgive?" Lydia questioned, not even responding to Naomi's words. "Is this not stressed?"

"*Yah*, of course," her sister snapped, "but not that long ago, this Daniel was shunned! He rejected our life for the *Englischer* world. How can you be sure of him?"

"We cannot talk further of this now," Lydia said in a repressive voice as the room filled around them. "And we don't need to talk of it at all, if you cannot see that all must be forgiven to those who have repented. I am marrying Daniel. It is decided."

With that terse statement, she turned away to gesture to Anna Lehman. "Come! Sit with us. Are you getting to know everyone here?"

"*Goedemorgen*, Lydia and Naomi!" The younger woman took the chair next to Lydia. "*Yah*, I am staying with Mercy's *familye* here."

Aware that Naomi was uncharacteristically quiet as Lydia and Anna spoke, Lydia placed her hand over her sister's, gripping it a little. Even if she was taking an action of which her *Schweschder* didn't approve, she still loved her and wanted Naomi to come to accept her marriage.

"Of course! A very fine, friendly bunch are the Yoders," Lydia said, chatting on with the girl about whom all she'd met in Elizabethtown. As their conversation moved on, however, a part of her mind wrestled with Naomi's words.

Was she selfish to marry a *Mann* in Daniel's situation? Could her *Schweschder* be right? Maybe this wasn't fair to anyone, even to Daniel. Perhaps it would be more loving to allow her child to be raised by Cousin Rachel than to bring the *Boppli* into what might be turbulent waters if Daniel married her and went back to his

Englischer inclinations. Having so stumbled, she trembled with self-doubt.

"...and Mary Yoder has been so kind. Welcoming me into their home, even though I'm just a relative of Mercy's new husband through marriage."

"I am sure they're glad to have you stay," Naomi finally spoke to assure the girl.

"And have you met the younger *Menner* here?" Lydia asked with a smile, still mentally wrestling with her own dilemma.

Daniel didn't seem to her as if he were unsure of his choice and he was adamant about the *Boppli* being their child. He had admittedly done a very disturbing thing—she still didn't understand why he'd done it—but it took strength of character to return and face his consequences.

It might not have made sense to Naomi, but even though she doubted herself, Lydia felt she could trust him despite his past actions.

"Come, *Buwe*," Daniel called to Mark a few days later. He slapped Barley's russet rump with affection before going back to climb in the relative warmth afforded by the buggy.

"What?" Mark looked up from the leather he'd been cleaning. "Why?"

"Because I want you to come with me to run this errand." Daniel gave his words a lazy drawl. If his time with the boy was to be helpful in anyway, Mark must not see it as anything, but casual.

The bishop's grandson didn't get up from his place beside the bucket of water, damp leather stretched out in front of him. "I'll stay here. I have to finish this."

"It'll wait," Daniel said, "Looks like you've slopped enough soapy water on the leather for it to need some time to dry. Besides, that looks like cold work. Come with me."

"Joel told me to clean it." Mark's words were sullen.

"Yes, he did," Daniel agreed, saying nothing more. He sat on the buggy seat and looked steadily at Mark.

"Okay." With evident bad-temper, Mark dropped the sponge he'd been using into a bucket, getting up as he scrubbed his wet hands dry before walking around to the buggy's passenger seat. "I don't know why you need me to go."

"It is a question," Daniel agreed, flicking the reins lightly to get the horse moving through the crisp air. "It smells as if snow is coming again this afternoon."

The boy mumbled an unintelligible reply which Daniel decided to ignore.

They trotted along in silence for a few minutes before Mark grumbled in a sour voice. "You can't need me. I'm just a peewee next to you and Joel. Abel's even lots bigger than me."

"*Yah.*"

"I can't be of any help in lifting anything heavy or fixing a buggy wheel."

"*Neh*, probably not." Daniel made no other response than the upward quirk of one side of his mouth. Although he'd never been as open about his discontent, he'd often felt just as impatient as Mark.

"Well, why did you make me come then?" the boy demanded as their buggy trotted along the russet tree-lined lane.

"Ever consider I might just want your good company?" Daniel slanted a glance to his side with a smile.

"I doubt that," Mark snapped, "and I don't see what you're laughing at."

Daniel's smile widened. "I didn't know I was laughing."

They continued to ride along in the buggy not speaking, the fall countryside passing. Here and there, trees held leaves still, all gold and brown. The air smelled cold and crisp with just a hint of a distant fireplace.

"You have been working in Joel's shop pretty much every day," Daniel finally commented without expression.

"*Yah.*" Mark said resentfully.

"Why is a *youngie* like yourself not in school? Did you race to finish already?"

"You know I haven't."

Chuckling as he held the buggy horse reins loosely, Daniel said, "You must think your *Grossdaddi* and I talk about you a lot. All I know about you is that you don't go to school. That's why you work at Joel's."

"I don't know what you and *Grossdaddi* talk about." Mark's words were low and filled with his usual simmering anger.

"Well, we don't talk about everything." Steering Barley through a turn, Daniel lapsed into silence.

"Well, what do you talk with *Grossdaddi* about then?" The words eventually burst from the boy. "You and he talk all the time."

"*Yah*, we do, but not about you." Daniel wondered if his *Eldre* had known how often he was angry. Like Mark, he'd had older *Geschwischders* and one younger. When there were a lot of children in a family, the silent ones sometimes got lost, he supposed.

"What do you talk about then? You and *Grossdaddi*?" Mark blurted out the question again, not seeming to realize it was nosey.

"Me, mostly," Daniel returned with a tremor of a grin. "And all my mistakes and poor choices."

The slight figure beside him made no response to this admission at first. Then Mark turned, asking in a curious voice, as if he'd never thought much about it before, "What mistakes and poor choices?"

Driving now down a gravel lane, Daniel turned the buggy in at a gate that led to a pasture. "What you and I spoke of before. I lost my way for a while and am now finding it again."

"Oh," Mark said, staring as Daniel climbed down from the buggy seat to open the pasture gate. "Why did you come back? It had to be hard. I don't know why anyone would return after the church members shunned him."

He sounded irritated and puzzled, staring as Daniel got back into the buggy, clucking at the horse to move through the now-opened gate. Here and there, clumps of fall leaves huddled around trees and off to the side of the gate a young yearling stood, watching them with large, cautious eyes, its coat a dark charcoal.

"*Yah*," Daniel glanced over at the boy, feeling sadness seep a little into his expression, "it had to be done. I knew I belonged here. Like a prodigal, *Gott* spoke to me and I returned. Even though it was hard. Staying away was harder."

"Why?" Mark seemed indignant. "Why were you shunned?"

Pulling back on the reins to halt the buggy, Daniel said, "As I have said, I went seriously astray and the shunning was to protect the others in the church flock."

"Did you beat up someone here?"

"*Neh*, but I deserted the girl I was to marry and ran off to the *Englischer* world for a time." Daniel moved around to the front of the buggy horse that stood now in front a watering trough, ignoring the boy's startled face. "Now *youngie* Mark, I have job for you."

"You said something about this before. You lived in the *Englischer* world?" Mark was clearly so caught up in Daniel's youthful dilemma that he didn't attend to his latter words.

"*Yah*, but enough of that. Do you see young Apple over there by the fence?"

The boy glanced to where Daniel pointed, climbing slowly down from the buggy. "That colt? *Yah*. I see him."

"Well, he's your job now. You are to come here every day to feed and water him…and to talk to him."

Mark swiveled to look at Daniel. "Talk to him? About what?"

Daniel shrugged, still watching the foal. "Anything you like. But you must do this every day. Several times every day. And you must stay and visit a while each day with Apple, until he gets used to you. Used to you enough that he lets you start grooming him."

He knew that like other *youngies*, Mark was accustomed to helping with the animals around his *Eldre's* farm. "Apple is skittish. He was with his *Mamm* for a while, but she took sick and died. Now Apple's having a hard time getting used to people. He needs you to be his friend."

Mark said nothing, staring at the young horse.

"Apple belongs to Joel and so this will be part of your job. You are to work some in the buggy shop, but mostly you are to be Apple's friend."

Still saying nothing, the boy watched the yearling.

"I made some mistakes before when I ran away to the *Englischer* world, young Mark," Daniel said. "Think carefully before you make big mistakes. Tell Apple all about everything. He will come to understand."

Mark swiveled back, to point out. "He's a horse."

"Apple is one of *Gott's* creations, perhaps an angel in disguise. Whether he is or not, he's lost his way, too. Mayhap you can help one another."

CHAPTER SIX

"I'm only three years younger than my youngest *Bruder*," Mark finally muttered as they clip-clopped in the buggy behind the horse after leaving the field where the colt lived, "but they won't let me do things. It's like they think I'm still a little kid."

Daniel glanced over. This was the first his young companion had spoken since they left the young foal's pasture. He didn't know why he resonated with this dark boy. Daniel had enough troubles of his own, even if Lydia had agreed to marry him. He had no issue with her already being with child. He looked forward to having a *Boppli* of his own, but he knew there still remained some in the church who mistrusted him. When he'd foolishly rejected their life, they'd turned their backs on him. They weren't sure yet that he could be trusted.

Daniel sighed, knowing *Gott* had forgiven him and wondering when he would be able to do that himself.

He and the boy drove along in silence a while before Daniel offered, "Sounds like all older *Bruders*. They seem to always look down on the younger. I have three, myself. And three sisters, two of them are older, as well."

"Always bossing, like they know anything," Mark groused with disgust. "Like I can't do anything since I'm younger than they are. I finally got tired of it."

"*Yah*?" Daniel looked at him with amused curiosity. "What did you do?"

The boy swallowed, his normally glowering expression becoming more mutinous. "Nothing. Not really. My *Eldre* didn't do anything about them, either. Even though I told them how it was."

"So you took matters into your own hands," Daniel concluded when Mark didn't answer what he'd done.

"I did." Mark turned a stormy face his way.

"Did you let all the pigs out of their pen when it was one of your *Bruders'* job to take care of them? Or steal all the eggs from under the hens?"

"No… I-I set a hay bale on fire." The admission was made both defiantly and fearfully, as if grownups had shouted at him about this before. "It wasn't a big bale and there were no buildings around it to catch fire."

Slanting another glance at Mark, Daniel maintained his calm expression. "And how was this to show your *Bruders* you were grown?"

Mark's response was even more sullen as he spoke downward to his lap. "It was in the field where my oldest *Bruder*, Aaron, had been working. I guess—I guess I wanted to get back at him. He never lets me go along anywhere with him!"

Slowing the horse to make another turn, Daniel accomplished this before asking, "How did you get caught? How did they know it was you that set fire to your *Bruder's* hay bale?"

"Aaron and Josiah saw me."

"Dang. That was bad luck." Clucking at the horse to make a turn, Daniel didn't bother keeping the sympathy out of his voice. Mark's infraction was severe and Daniel knew his punishment would have been, too.

The boy had acted out in a destructive manner… Daniel could only feel compassion for that.

"*Denki* for letting me help with your wedding dress," Anna said shyly that same day. "I hadn't heard that you and Daniel Stoltzfus were to marry."

Lydia tried to control her blush. This kind of remark would be made often, she knew, and with greater slyness. Shock, too, since Daniel wasn't yet accepted by many.

"You're certainly welcome. Since he came to work for my *Daed*, we have been thrown together more." She smiled at the *Maedel*, shifting the subject. "I heard that Mercy's *Mamm* has kept you quite busy. I'm glad you had time to help."

"Since the weather has grown colder, she has only a very few rows in the garden," Anna replied, her head in her black *kapp* bent over the fabric they were cutting.

"How is your visit here going?" Now that she was using the herbs Daniel had procured from Mercy for her, Lydia was beginning to feel better. She shifted her scissors to make a better cut.

He was more kind to her than she'd expected since their marriage was to be one of convenience, although there had been no more damp sheet episodes.

"It is well." Anna's brow wrinkled with concentration as she, too, moved around the fabric spread on the floor. "I love this particular blue fabric. It will look well on you."

"The color of the sky as evening comes. One of the glories *Gott* gives us," Lydia smiled, realizing she'd unmindfully quoted Daniel.

"*Yah.* It will serve you nicely for Sunday wear after you are married."

"This is the plan." Lydia threaded a needle. "Tell me about the *Buwe* you like best. Do you have a favorite here?"

Her young friend blushed again. "*Neh.* They are all silly. I mean all of them, both here and at home."

Lydia remembered the sorting-out days when all young *Menner* were silly and all were possibilities. Hiding a smile, she asked, "Are any of them sillier than the rest?"

"I think Abel Schrock is annoying. I'm sorry. I know he works for your *Daed*." The girl lifted a piece of fabric she'd cut for the dress skirt.

Not bothering to respond to this, Lydia invited, "What annoying things does Abel do?"

Anna waved a dismissive hand. "He's always talking about his buggy and his buggy horse. Saying his *Daed* plans to buy him a farm soon. Like I care."

Directing a grin at the fabric in front of her, Lydia said, "How annoying. I wonder why he thinks you would care about those things."

"I have no idea," Anna responded disdainfully before quickly smiling. "Did I tell you that Mercy and Isaac are traveling through next week before heading back to Mannheim? We will see them because they plan to stop for the night at her *Mamm's* and *Daed's*."

"How nice!"

The smile Anna shot her way looked pinched. "It will be nice to see them, but I wish I was returning with them. I miss my *Mamm*."

Lydia's heart lurched within her. "I'll bet you do miss your *Mamm* a lot, but you must remember that you'll go home and see her soon."

At least, Anna was safe in the Yoder *Haus*, not exposed to unprotected isolation a girl could face during *rumspringa* far from *familye*. Lydia knew only too well what that kind of loneliness could drive a *Maedel* to do.

If she hadn't been so lonely on her *rumspringa*, would she be marrying Daniel now? What strange paths life took.

Later that afternoon, the warm stove in the buggy shop hissed quietly as Daniel worked alone, carefully fitting another new spoke into the shattered wheel of a nearby wounded buggy.

When the shop door opened suddenly, he looked up. Joel and Abel had gone together to bring in a break down. Since Mark was spending a day with his *Grossdaddi*, Daniel expected no visitors.

He half expected that Lydia might take a break from working on her wedding dress to visit with him and he turned a smiling face to greet her.

But the burly figure standing just inside the door that swung closed against the cold wasn't Lydia.

The smile on Daniel's face slowly stiffened as his father removed the broad snow-sprinkled hat from his gray head.

With his usual harsh expression, he glared at Daniel fiercely, Jeremiah's cheeks reddened by the cold. "*der Suh*."

Accustomed to his father not showing any different expression, Daniel made no comment on it now.

"*Daed*." Feeling the familiar clutch of grief and anger mixed now with guilt, he braced his frame and smiled politely at his father before refocusing on the wheel in his hands.

"Hello," the older *Mann* responded, nodding his graying head at his son.

"Come in," Daniel invited, jerking his head toward the stove. "Warm yourself."

Having drawn off knit gloves that were an improbable scarlet, Jeremiah Stoltzfus went to the potbellied stove, bracing his broad hat under one arm and rubbing his hands as he held them out to the warmth.

Jeremiah was a large *Mann*, his barrel chest making him seem even more imposing. He turned back from the heat to ask in his ever-annoyed tone, "How are you doing here?"

Blowing on the spoke hole to clear out the shavings he'd been boring, Daniel didn't respond immediately. "I am fine. Joel has been more than kind and I like this work."

"*Gut*."

Silence followed his father's single word, only the stove's hissing and crackling filling the space as Daniel whittled at the base of the wheel spoke. He wasn't surprised that his father was here, but he wouldn't have been surprised it there had been no visit, either.

Finally, Jeremiah Stoltzfus cleared his throat. "Your *Mamm* tells me you are to marry, that you and Joel's *Dochder*, Lydia, will soon wed. She is the older girl? Lydia? The only one left at home?"

"She is." Daniel knew that when he'd gone to his old home to tell his *Eldre* of his marriage and found only his *Mamm* there that his father would learn from her of their son's planned marriage. In truth, he hadn't even been sure Jeremiah would speak to him of it.

"*Yah*," he said now, setting his small wood chisel down as he met his *Daed's* gaze. "I am a very fortunate *Mann*. Lydia is a wonderful, kind, godly woman. I believe I will be very happy with her. We will have purposeful, worshipful lives together."

His stern expression not changing, Jeremiah nodded. "You are fortunate. To have such an unblemished *Maedel* agree to marry you after your actions the past year. Well, that has to be *Gott's* blessing."

Daniel drew in a deep breath. It didn't even occur to him to respond to his father's designation of Lydia...or to respond to the implied insult toward himself. Saying why she was marrying him didn't even occur to him. Not for anything would he expose Lydia to anyone's scorn, certainly not that of his unyielding parent.

As for himself, he knew he'd chosen this path.

"I believe I am fortunate...and also that Lydia is *Gott's* blessing to me," he said. "I only hope that I can be close to as great a blessing to her. I also hope that you and *Mamm*—and all my *Geschwischder*—will pray for the success of our union."

"I am certain we will." His father repositioned his hat on his gray head. "Well, I must be going now. I believe your *Mamm* is making stew for supper and the days grow shorter now."

"I'm glad you came by," Daniel offered as Jeremiah walked to the buggy shop door.

"*Yah*. You and Lydia must come have supper with your *Mamm* and me after you're wed." With that—and a stiff nod—his father went out.

Daniel looked at the door through for a long moment, committing to himself and *Gott* to be a more accessible *Daed* to his own *Kinder*. There was no doubt that he'd made many, many errors in his life—and would likely make many more—but he wanted his own children to always know that they were loved and they could come to him. He'd make sure of that.

Being a loving *Daed* and a *gut* husband was his greatest prayer.

On the following Thursday, Daniel—wearing his new black wedding suit with its special bow tie and Lydia, beautiful in her new blue dress and black wedding cape next to him—stood before the bishops and the church congregation to marry in traditional plain fashion.

"As you both, Daniel Stoltzfus and Lydia Troyer have both been baptized into the church and your plan to marry was published before the congregation, is it your wish that we draw together this morning to formalize your union before *Gott*?"

"*Yah*." Uttering his response in a strong, sure voice, Daniel glanced at Lydia. With her wide smile, she was beautiful standing next to him. He vowed silently again to make her a *gut* husband. No matter how they'd been lead to this, they could be happy together. He had no doubt.

"*Yah*."

Beside him with glowing dark eyes, Lydia stood there in a white *kapp*, wearing a matching white organdy apron over her new blue dress. The accessories of a married *Frau*.

Under her *kapp*, the smooth wings of dark hair framed her sweet face and Daniel sent up to *Gott* a brief prayer of thanks. He'd never expected to be so lucky at this point in his foolish life to have had such a kind woman standing to take her vows beside him.

And one that made him laugh, too, in her sillier moments. He didn't deserve Lydia.

Daniel knew that this was typically a day of mixed anxiety and excitement for most *Menner*, but he felt only joy. The past year had been tumultuous and painful for him. When he'd returned to his bed in the *Englischer* world after sneaking into Mannheim to speak to Mercy—the woman he'd jilted when he ran away to that life—he'd faced complete despair.

Mercy naturally had no interest in running off to join him in that world and he recognized now that he'd only wanted this so he wouldn't face his terrifying choice alone.

The months that had followed had been difficult—like the Prodigal Son's time in the pig sty—but those moments of struggle had led him to return to his life here. And the conviction that this was the exact spot *Gott* had chosen for him had only grown since Lydia had agreed to marry him.

He was even happier working with Joel in the buggy shop than he had been working his *Daed's* fields. Being here suited him.

Daniel looked down at Lydia beside him. He'd sat beside her earlier as the minister counseled them in a back bedroom, his chest feeling heavy with the weight of the responsibilities that came with their union. It was not a bad feeling, but he still struggled to feel worthy. He'd now have a *familye* for whom he was fully responsible and *Kinder* who would look up to him, relying on him for guidance. Soon, he and Lydia would have a wonderful *Boppli* to cradle. While he welcomed this with joy, he faced the truth of this responsibility. He would represent *Gott* to his children and be a loving mate to Lydia. He had to be fully the *Mann* he knew she deserved and the *Daed* their infant deserved.

Hoping fervently that he could be this, Daniel prayed again for forgiveness.

His own father was a strong *Mann* and *gut* in *Gott's* eyes...but he wasn't a soft *Mann*.

Daniel knew he was so unworthy.

Out of her kindness, Lydia had chosen to have only one attendant—her sister, Naomi. Daniel knew she'd done this since he only had his one *Bruder* as attendant with him. Lydia's *Schweschder* wore an appropriately serious expression, mirroring John's, the only *Bruder* Daniel had asked to stand beside him. John was closest to him in age, although two sisters had been born into the *familye* between them. Daniel had shared more adventures with John than with his older *Bruders*.

And still, he hadn't talked with John about his own struggles before charging off into the *Englischer* world. He wasn't even sure what to say about any of that.

It had all been pride, he recognized now, and a lack of faith. Returned to his home with his tail between his legs, he knew they were none good enough for *Gott's* grace. They all needed *Gott* to make up the difference.

And his need was even greater.

Daniel drew a deep breath before releasing it slowly. He'd been such a fool...

It troubled, but did not surprise him, to see the dark, broken expression in John's eyes still whenever his *Bruder* looked at him. Daniel did not doubt, though, that John and the rest of his family forgave him. Such was directed by *Gott* and even though the words of forgiveness had been freely offered him by his *Eldre* and *Geschwischder*, it was only natural that his having abandoned them and his life here had left damage.

Daniel sent up a silent prayer of thanks that John now stood next to him at this moment. In a row of chairs placed for the congregation sat Daniel's *Mamm* and *Daed*. Although he knew his *Eldre* would witness his wedding—as they would any other in the church—it still choked him up to make these vows with them as witnesses.

One day they would be convinced that he recognized the error of his ways. Mayhap then they would feel...safer...to rely on him.

"And in this marriage," Bishop Fisher spoke now directly to Lydia, "will you cleave to this *Mann* as the head of your household and give him comfort through the challenges we face in this world?"

"*Yah*, I will." Her response was prompt and definite.

Although it wasn't usually difficult to hold in private his thoughts and feelings, Daniel found himself tearing a little as a smile spread across his face at the solid conviction in Lydia's words. She had minimal reason to have faith in him, even though he took this step knowing all she brought with her.

She could have taken the easier road and given her *Boppli* to her aunt. In many ways, that would have been the simplest path. Still, she plighted her troth to him.

"It is nice to see you again, Lydia." Daniel's *Mamm* smiled, nodding at her across the supper table a week later. In between Daniel's work in her *Daed's* buggy shop they were making post-wedding visits with as many as they could. While at the other visits, occasional strained motherly smiles were thrown Daniel's way, none of their visits had included as awkward a meal as the one to which they sat down now.

Jeremiah Stoltzfus sat at the head of the supper table, his stern face never relaxing as he ate.

Despite that, Daniel hadn't given up his sometimes-stilted conversation with the older *Mann*.

"And you, *Frau* Stoltzfus." Lydia returned his mother's smile. She'd grown up knowing the older Stoltfuses and all their children. "How are Leah and Rebecca doing? I haven't seen either since they moved away after marrying."

"Oh, *yah*, they are fine." Ada Stoltzfus beamed. "You have probably heard that Leah had twin *Bopplis* last spring and Rebecca is settling in fine to being a *Frau*."

"I did hear about Leah's twins," Lydia responded before spooning in another bite. She couldn't help compare this tense meal to some of the others they'd shared recently with friends and neighbors, but then she supposed it was more difficult when one's own child went astray.

Nevertheless, she had to give Daniel credit. He listened attentively to his father's occasional utterances, nodding seriously when Jeremiah spoke of the crops that were being planted in land Lydia knew had always been promised to Daniel.

After more stilted conversation, the meal finally ended and she got up to help Ada clear and wash the dishes. It was almost comforting to do this familiar thing, an act she'd been helping her own *Mamm* with since she was small. Of course, then there had been sisters to help amid cheerful chatter.

This was nothing like clean-up after their *familye* meals.

Aware that Daniel had shifted to sit with his father to a bench near the fireplace while she and his *Mamm* washed up, Lydia sent up a prayer of thanks again for the herbal concoction he'd gotten for her from Mercy. Without out it, she might have been overcome by the smells of lingering food and dirty dishes and had to run outside into the chilly night to lose her supper.

Morning sickness, indeed.

"I want to thank you, Lydia." Ada Stoltzfus handed her a soapy plate to rinse, her voice low. "For, you know, marrying Daniel."

"Thank me?" The oddity of the woman's words surprised her.

"*Yah*." Daniel's *Mamm* looked briefly over her shoulder to where he sat with his father by the fire. "I know my Daniel hasn't always lived a simple, plain life in *Gott*. He—he is considered a risk by some."

The smile she sent Lydia was tight. "We are to forgive. It is *Gott's* way. But the very human part of others can make this difficult. Particularly when…"

"When a *Mann* has done what many *Eldre* are fearful their own *Kinder* will do," Lydia finished, keeping her words as low as Ada's.

"*Yah*." The older woman sent another flickering glance toward the fireplace. "We are to forgive, but no one said this would be easy."

Frau Stolztfus glanced over, a faint tinge of curiosity in her eyes. "I am grateful you were willing to see Daniel's good qualities."

Later as Lydia and Daniel made the buggy drive back to his sparse room, she reflected on this unsettling conversation. While it was a relief that he hadn't told his *Eldre* about her being with child, she couldn't help feeling troubled by the visit.

"Daniel?"

He glanced over, holding the buggy reins relaxed in his big hands. "*Yah.*"

"Your *Daed*... He has always been quiet and...hard to read. As long as I've known him, anyway."

"*Yah.*" Daniel's voice was indifferent, which seemed jarring considering the subject they discussed.

"As I watched you tonight," she said, turning it over in her mind, "it occurs to me that this might have—"

"*Yah?*"

"Might have made it...difficult to...to feel his love when you were a *Scholar.*" The last part of her sentence came out in a rush as she realized in the middle of it that this was an awkward subject. Even though she'd married Daniel and now shared the intimacies of married life, she wondered if this subject was off limits.

Daniel didn't say anything for a few moments, merely staring ahead at the now dusky road they traveled down.

Finally, the *Mann* she'd married turned his face to her and said, "He did his best, my *Daed*. He may be difficult to read, but I...I never doubted that he loved us."

Feeling a little reprimanded, she sat next to him, also staring ahead without saying anything before she turned to him finally. "It...must have been difficult, though. You're *Daed* is...is nothing like Bishop Fisher. Or my *Daed.*"

"*Neh,*" Daniel agreed finally as if closing a door with a slam. "He's not."

Nothing more was said, the silence between them uncomfortable.

The last few days after the ceremony had been filled with a flurry of activity. Lydia's things were moved to Daniel's small room off the buggy shop...and then there had been visits to make between his times working in her *Daed's* shop.

Although she now shared her husband's room and his bed, Lydia still felt there was much to learn about him.

"You must let me help! We don't know how long it will be before it gets even colder out here," Lydia protested for the third time from her seat on the stump at the corner of the Troyer vegetable garden the next morning.

Knowing sitting by unoccupied was hard for her, Daniel shook his head, sending Lydia a mock-stern glance. They were alone in the garden plot that was tucked close behind the *Haus*. The afternoon sun was keeping away the worst of the chill, but it was still fall.

"If you must be out here, you could bring some of your sewing to occupy your hands," he suggested.

"I don't think so." She shook her head. "It's too cool for my bare fingers to work right and, besides, the material might fall to the ground and get dirty."

"*Yah*, it might." He'd been so tense the evening before when taking her to have supper with his *Eldre*, but Lydia had been…just right. Warm and friendly to his *Mamm*. Respectful with his silent *Daed*, even though she'd remarked about him afterwards.

She'd been all that could be expected of an actual loving spouse, even if she had spoken questions later of what she couldn't understand.

From his spot in the earthy row of beets, he looked up at her. Why had he not noticed her all those years before?

"Woman," he said in his mock stern tone, gesturing toward her, "sit back down on that tree stump or I'll—"

"You'll what?"

She sent him a shy, faintly-teasing look. Startled with the urge to catch his bride in his arms and assure her that she was safe now, Daniel bent again to the task of pulling the last of the root vegetables out of the chilly ground. Of course, her *Mamm* possibly looking out the kitchen window and her *Daed* being in the buggy shop nearby kept him from acting in a way that might scandalize them both.

In truth, it startled him, too.

Up to this point, he'd tried hard to be the respectable, reliable *Mann* Bishop Fisher believed him to be, but he found that Lydia made this hard. She'd thrown her lot in with his and that still amazed him. Most of the people he'd grown up with still viewed him with strong caution. He'd left the church and all with which he'd grown up. Although he knew she was in a desperate situation, he was so glad every day that Lydia had trusted him enough to become his *Frau*.

"You'll do what if I don't sit here?" she asked again, her generous smile still spread across her face.

"You don't want to know," he told her in a repressive tone that made her laugh. Smiling at the sound, he thrust his hands in again to yank out a root vegetable. It was no surprise that he hadn't attended to Lydia Troyer's charms before this. He'd been too tangled up in his own pride, his blind march toward marriage with Mercy… His own sense of not being enough.

"I'm not scared of you, Daniel," she responded, her grin peeping out to daring him. "You're just a softy and I know the truth about you now."

"*Frau* Stoltzfus, do not hinder me from gathering the harvest from the fall garden," he cautioned her, his responding smile aimed at the rows still yet to be harvested.

"I have told you over and over that I'm fine to do this myself," she protested mildly, shaking her head at him with that same kind smile.

Blessed be to *Gott* for having led him Lydia's way. He had unquestioningly taken the hard path—like Jonah in the Good Book—but it warmed him to his toes that he hadn't ended up in the belly of a whale. Instead, *Gott* had made use of Lydia's sad dilemma to send Daniel into her warm arms.

Daniel didn't understand any of this, but he was deeply grateful.

CHAPTER SEVEN

"I think we should call the *Boppli* after Hiram, your father's old worker."

Later that day, Lydia and Daniel sat down to supper at a small makeshift table in the corner of his room. While the new couple had eaten with her *Mamm* and *Daed* in the family house up till now, Lydia's *Eldre* were eating tonight with friends.

She now huffed a sound between laughter and disgust. "Don't be ridiculous."

Every now and then the serious *Mann* she'd married had a silly moment. She had to admit she liked it despite that his dry humor still startled her. He was normally so contained.

They still hadn't talked more about what had led to his leaving the Amish world or his return to it and Lydia wasn't sure how to ask about the topic. Although he wasn't the least bit forbidding, she got a strong sense that some subjects were off limits...like when she'd spoken of his *Daed*.

"Hiram, particularly," he continued with a mock serious expression, "if it's a girl *Boppli*."

Hearing the teasing sound in his voice, she laughed. "*Yah*, but only if it's a girl."

Daniel grinned. "Or we could call her Tirzah. I believe this means 'pleasing' in Hebrew if I remember right. It was used in the Bible book Judges."

For all that they'd been married over two weeks now and shared the same close living quarters, Lydia still felt a little shy when they were alone. Although she'd grown up with him and had seen his hard, cheerful work alongside her *Daed* in the buggy shop, Lydia reflected that she really still knew little about the *Mann* she'd married and now slept beside.

Not really.

Even though the group of children in their community hadn't been large, she and Daniel had hung out with different friends. Honestly, she hadn't previously given much thought to him or how he got along with his *Eldre*, but their meal the other night had seemed...strained. Of course *Eldre* always worried about their *Kinder* and suffered alongside them. Daniel's having left for the *Englischer* world would have been very hard on his parents.

She'd expected more...welcoming of the prodigal, though, now that he'd returned to the fold.

"I don't actually think," Lydia said now, chuckling as she considered Daniel's words, "that's what we should call the *Boppli*, even if it should be a girl."

He smiled before lifting his fork. "Maybe Rufus then?"

Lydia just shook her head as she laughed. "Let's consider other names, although it's early to talk of these."

"If you say so," Daniel conceded with a slight smile.

Lydia started gathering the dishes from the table.

"Daniel," she kept stacking, "tell me about why you left Elizabethtown."

She looked up, meeting his gaze steadily.

He shifted back in his chair, dropping his eyes to the table before he finally answered. "There's really nothing to say. I was...prideful and very mistaken. I finally realized that. You need not worry. I will never again seek treasure in the *Englischer* world. I know the only path is through *Gott*."

Reaching across the small table, he to grasp her hand. "I promise, Lydia, that I will always remain faithful to *Gott*, our *Boppli* and you. You do not need to worry."

Exchanging a steady glance across the table with her hand in his grasp, she thought again that he still faced many who doubted his sincerity.

"I know that, Daniel." She looked down, pulling her hand free to continue to stack the dishes. "I wouldn't have married you if I didn't believe this."

Although, she'd scooted back her chair to stand, she paused. "That isn't what I asked you, however. I sat at the table with your *Mamm* and *Daed* last night. And I wondered…"

At the mention of his *Eldre* Daniel's face took on the shuttered look she'd noticed before. "Wondered what?"

She lifted the stack of dirty dishes, carrying them to a small sink in the corner of the room before swinging back to him.

"Daniel, I am your wife now."

He maintained a stoic expression, looking at her. "*Yah.*"

"I could have married old Peter Stromeyer." She shrugged to acknowledge the ridiculousness of that option and said, "but I have entrusted myself and my *Boppli* in you."

"*Yah*, you have," his gaze dropped again to the table in front of him, "and I will never let down either you or our child."

"I did not marry you lightly." She placed the dishes in the sink, turning back to say, "As you know, I could have given my *Boppli* to my *Aenti*… The *Boppli* would have been loved and safe there."

"I know." His words were a little impatient.

She stood beside the sink. "But…I felt in my heart that you would be a good husband to me and a loving father to the *Boppli*."

"I know and I will. You were right about this. I already love the child. It is my determination that he or she will know this." He sounded firm now, his words strong. "You have entrusted yourself to me, Lydia. I promise I will not let you down."

It struck her then that Daniel felt he'd let down many others and that—which made his promise about the *Boppli* all the more poignant—that he'd not always been sure of his *Daed's* love.

"Then, perhaps, you can eventually talk with me about…everything. About why you left for the *Englischer* world and didn't marry Mercy. And maybe someday, you can…tell your father you'd like his love."

He drew a long breath, looking down at the table, but said nothing more.

"You want me to drive you to the Glick farm?" Daniel asked Lydia the next day. It was foolish. He had repented of his pridefulness and mistaken thoughts, but the farm was still associated in his mind with that disastrous summer of his abortive *rumspringa* and the foolish, heart-wrenching things he'd said to Isaac Miller.

"*Yah*," she said, looking over her shoulder at him with innocent unawareness. "Anna wants me there when she says goodbye to Mercy and Isaac. They are stopping by to speak to *Frau* Glick on their way back home. She wasn't here when they passed this way last."

His young wife leaned against the buggy he'd been working on. Her *Daed* and Abel could be heard from where they worked at the other end of the buggy shop. Lydia said, "I think that even though Anna likes *Frau* Yoder—Mercy's *Mamm*, you know— she's a little nervous of staying here after Mercy and Isaac return to Mannheim."

"I expect Mercy and Isaac will be glad to get back home, at last." Daniel looked down to where he was scrubbing the last spots of grease off his hands, saying without inflection, "Of course, I'll drive you, Lydia. It's no trouble."

Lydia hesitated then and he could feel her gaze. There had been a faint new undercurrent of strain since she asked about his having left the faith. She said now in a self-conscious voice, "I'm sorry. I can take the buggy myself. No need for you to bother yourself."

Daniel looked up quickly, seeing her flush. "*Neh*. I truly don't mind."

Smiling faintly, he added, "Your stomach might bother you, making you need to stop. I will come with...and steady the horse that probably isn't accustomed to those sounds."

Lydia glanced up to meet his smiling gaze before responding. "I-I haven't been sick in several weeks. Are you sure you can come? I don't want to-to force you to speak to Mercy and Isaac, if it makes you uncomfortable. I mean, you already asked Mercy for those herbs to settle my stomach. It was probably awkward."

Straightening from his work stool, Daniel came to stand close to her, saying in a low voice as he put his hand over the one she rested on the buggy. "*Neh*, it was not awkward. You needed the concoction. Mercy is nothing to me now, but an old friend. It's truly not a problem for me to see her, Lydia. Where she is concerned, I have no regrets. I will gladly take you to the Glick farm to see Anna and Mercy and Isaac."

Lydia glanced up at him, asking softly, "You don't have any regrets?"

"None about not marrying Mercy." He spoke with certainty. "Not about marrying you. I have regrets, Lydia. Many of them. But not about that...and not about our *Boppli*. I very much look forward to being a *Daed*."

She looked up and met his steady gaze and he saw the lingering self-doubt in her eyes. Ever since she'd mentioned wanting him to confide in her, Daniel had fought to find the words.

It was important to him not to excuse his wrongful actions...and he struggled to know how to talk about his childhood or his *Eldre*. Those were waters he preferred to avoid altogether. She'd grown up with Miriam and Joel. What could she know of the life he'd had?

He said with difficulty, "I was... I was a prideful, foolish *Buwe*, Lydia, and I made bad choices, but I am convinced that marrying you—and starting a *familye* with you—was absolutely the right thing to do. Do you want to go to the Glick farm now?"

An hour later the buggy jogged down the lane in Daniel's buggy and they sat on the seat, their sleeves brushing. Ever since they'd talked that night after leaving his *Eldre's Haus*, he'd felt a hot bubble in his chest and it had only grown. He almost felt the hot bubble was blocking his breathing and the words he should have said.

Not sure what this was about, he now held the reins loosely in his hand, struggling with the frustration of not knowing his own mind.

He abruptly muttered, "This is a *gut* life, ours, and I wouldn't ever say my *Eldre* didn't do right by me."

Clearly startled, Lydia didn't respond immediately, just turning to send him a long look. "I don't believe I said they hadn't."

"*Neh*, you didn't," he agreed, lapsing into a frustrated silence. This subject made him uncomfortable. He was very aware of his own transgressions. Maybe that was why he was so relieved that Mercy had found Isaac.

He'd screwed up everything so badly. At least he hadn't messed up her life, as well as, his.

In perplexed concern, she sat next to Daniel. Lydia didn't at first attend to the flutter in her midsection. Their buggy trotted further down the road, the branches of tall oaks waving above them in the breeze.

Lydia didn't know how to ease the trouble she sensed in Daniel, but she wanted to help in some way.

It wasn't until she'd felt the flutter several times in roughly the same spot that she gasped in recognition.

"What? Did you forget something?" Daniel glanced over at her.

Almost unconsciously, she held her hand pressed to her midsection, overcome with a dawning sense of wonderment.

"Is your stomach upset?" He looked at her with concern. "Do you need to stop? I was only joking about the sounds. You need not worry about upsetting the horse—or me."

"Pull up," she quickly, knowing she said it in a strangled tone. "I'm not sick, but you must pull up."

He was already tugging on the reins to slow the horse, turning to her to ask in a concerned voice, "You're not sick? You know you need not feel embarrassed if you are."

Lydia drew in a shaky breath, holding his gaze. "Stop the horse. *Neh*, I'm not sick."

Doing as she asked he brought the horse to a standstill before crossing over a bridge in the road, glancing over to ask, "What is the problem? Have you changed your mind and don't want to go to the Glicks' farm after all? Are you not well?"

"It's not that, Daniel." She reached for his hand now that the buggy was stopped, placing the strong warmth of it on her midsection before urging in a hushed voice, "Feel!"

He looked at her with a startled expression.

"Just wait," she said in excitement, tears pricking behind her eyes. "Wait a moment and you'll feel it, too."

"I don't know," he said slowly. "You feel movement? From the *Boppli*?"

The excitement in his voice made her eyes even wetter.

"There," she said as the movement fluttered again. "There it is."

The startled expression on his face froze and then as the fluttering continued, a slow smile dawned. "That? That…little flicker? Is that what you mean?"

Lydia nodded, beaming at him with enthusiasm, "*Yah*! You feel it?"

"I—I do." His hand seemed to cup against her body, pressing a fraction closer. He looked up, his blue eyes seeming to have darkened when he looked up at her. "Is that our *Boppli*? You're sure?"

"*Neh*." Her laugh was shaky. "I'm not sure of anything, but I think that's what it is."

His hand was warm through the layers of her skirt. He held it pressed there against her, smiling up at her for several long moments before, he pulled back, seeming reluctant. "It is a miracle. *Gott's* miracle."

"*Yah*, it is," she agreed as he again lifted the reins to continue their journey.

Looking ahead at the road they trotted down—overhung with bare tree limbs—she smiled, thinking of having shared such a special moment with him.

They trotted on towards the Glick farm, a content silence having fallen between them.

Suddenly, Daniel turned away from the road, the broad hat on his head shifting as he looked her way. "My *Daed* and I...have always had this...complex interaction. We don't...get along very well."

At his unexpected words, she stared, waiting for him to continue. It was startling that he'd brought up the apparently-taboo subject now.

He turned back to the road. "I get along better with your *Daed*. Joel is such a kind *Mann*. Of all of us in my *familye*, *Daed* and I could never quite get on the same page. We argued."

"You and he didn't get along?" Lydia almost felt she was holding her breath, knowing instinctively that her husband didn't easily talk of this.

"*Neh*."

In the close confines of their buggy, she waited for him to continue. She felt...trusted and closer to him because Daniel brought up with her what was a difficult subject.

"I am the youngest son. The youngest child, but one." Daniel looked over at her again. He paused, his jaw seeming to tighten. "I will never—I will not treat our *Bopplis* as if they are not able to make their way in the world. As if they are..."

He seemed to grapple for the right word. "As if they are always wrong, if they don't agree. I am determined to listen to them, at least."

"Your *Daed* treated you this way?" she ventured. "As if he thought you—"

Daniel shook his head, finishing her question. "As if he thought I was damaged somehow. I don't know. We never shared a thought, never saw things the same way. He hung over me like I couldn't be trusted to do anything right on my own. Perhaps he was right."

Startled, she glanced over at him. "*Neh*, Daniel. Your *Daed* wasn't right."

He didn't respond to this remark, turning to look at her again before looking back at the road. "Have you not wondered why I of all the sons was to inherit my *Eldre's* farm? There are three *Buwes* older than I."

The thought had occurred to her, but such matters were often sorted out in the privacy of the *familye*.

"It was because my *Daed* thought I needed the help. I have three older *Bruders*, but I was to get the *Eldre's* farm because my *Daed* worried that I couldn't earn my own." Daniel's words came out in a tense voice.

Her response slipped out softly. "That must have been hard, to never agree with your *Daed*, to know he didn't believe in you."

"It was hard," Daniel agreed after a few moments, no inflection to his words, "but I wouldn't want anyone to think I blame my childhood for the mistakes I've made."

"You don't think…this had anything to do with it?" It was a hesitant question. She didn't see how this couldn't be at least a small part of Daniel's actions.

"*Neh*." His denial came out quickly. "I was a fool. A heedless, boasting, prideful fool. I must now rely on *Gott's* forgiveness of my unworthy self."

Just like that, he was through talking openly. It was as if a door had been slammed shut.

As they rounded the corner to Glick's farm, Lydia responded after a moment, "We must all be grateful for His forgiveness."

"Daniel! Daniel!" Mark came pelting around the shop door two mornings later. "Apple let me pet him!"

Wheeling around from the buggy on which he and Joel worked, Daniel grinned. "Did he really?"

"That's *gut, Youngie*," Joel said from where he squatted on the shop floor. "That colt needs a friend."

"He has the softest nose," the boy offered, his voice clear and anything but sullen. "I brought him some carrots every day, like you suggested, Daniel. And today when he took it from me, he let me pet his nose."

Smiling, Daniel handed Joel the wrench for which the older *Mann* reached. "You keep it up and Apple will soon come to trust people."

"I hope so." Mark sat on a nearby rolling stool, taking several extra carrots from under his broad hat. "Would you or Joel like one? They're fresh. I just pulled them from *Mamm's* garden this morning."

"You be careful, *youngie*, of pulling things from your *Mamm's* garden. There can't be much left this time of year." Joel grinned at the boy. "She might have been planning on those for supper."

"Oh, I asked her first," Mark assured him. "I'll be right back to work on cleaning out that storage room, but I go out first and wash my hands at the pump."

As he watched the boy speed out of the shop, Joel chuckled. "He's completely different. I think you are a *gut* influence on that *Buwe*."

He bent his graying head to the nut they worked to loosen. "Don't think I haven't noticed you speaking to him, taking him with you on errands and such."

Daniel shrugged, feeling his face warm slightly. "It isn't much."

"*Neh*," Joel disagreed, looking up. "It is. Sometimes we forget those younger and those who feel...displaced. Particularly when they're unpleasant."

"I don't think Mark means to be difficult," Daniel responded in a considering voice. "He's just..."

"A *Bensel*?"

"*Yah*. A silly child, but one also learning some of life's more harsh lessons," he agreed, glad Joel was tolerant and understanding.

"As have you learned," Joel concluded, giving him a level look as he put down the wrench he'd been using.

"Yes, I have."

Just then a shadow darkened the shop as Daniel's father, Jeremiah Stoltzfus, suddenly stepped in the door. "Daniel, I trust Joel is keeping you busy? *Gott* wants no idle hands."

Having looked up to see his *Daed's* broad form in the doorway, Daniel brushed his hands against his pants before formally offering his hand. "Daed. I'm glad you've come by. *Yah*, Joel is," he flashed a look at the *Mann* beside him, "very helpful."

To have his father come here again was…confusing, but it also left a small warmth in Daniel's chest. Although he'd often felt like a disappointment to Jeremiah—and he vowed never to convey this to his own son—it still meant a lot to have his father visit.

CHAPTER EIGHT

"Lydia," Naomi said the next day after they'd sewn in silence for a while, "I know you very well."

"Yah." Lydia wasn't sure where this was going, but Naomi clearly had something on her mind.

Her sister pulled to snap the thread she'd just tied off. "You aren't a push-over and *Mamm* and *Daed* have often remarked to me that I should be as *gut* as you."

Still bent over the seam she was stitching, Lydia slid her needle into the fabric with an ironic smile. "I doubt that will happen as often now."

"That's my point exactly." Naomi looked at her, the shirt in her *Schweschder's* lap apparently forgotten. "You are a strong-minded woman."

Her younger sister carefully rearranged the fabric. "This…this *Englischer* whose *Boppli* you carry, tell me about him."

Lydia didn't immediately respond, startled by the question. "The *Boppli* I carry is Daniel's and mine. What do you mean, who is the *Englischer*?"

"The question is perfectly clear. It's not a mystery," Naomi snapped. "You know to what I refer. You are to have a *Boppli*. This is why you married the heartbreaker, Daniel Stoltzfus, even if you wouldn't take old Peter Stromeyer. You married Daniel to keep and raise your *Boppli*. So, tell me about the father of this child."

"Oh. That's not the only reason I married Daniel, but I suppose…" Lydia started, stopped and then restarted, "I suppose

91

Brock was the best of a bad lot. Most of the *Englischers* I met while on *rumspringa* in Bedford weren't nice. They were loud and pushy, both drinking and smoking. But Brock... I don't believe—" She took up the shirt in her own lap and began stitching again. "I suppose he didn't mean me any harm."

"How could this be?" Naomi insisted. "You are carrying a child now because you—you laid with him. He left you in this way!"

They sat at a table across from the fireplace, especially kept for Lydia's sewing use. "Brock knows nothing of this. I never told him."

"What?" Her sister looked startled. "He doesn't know about the *Boppli*? Surely you said something about it to him."

"*Neh*. I didn't. I didn't realize the truth till I was home and..." Lydia straightened out the fabric to make sure the seam lay straight. "I knew Brock had plans for himself, that he was to start medical school soon. And it wasn't as if he and I ever made promises to one another or planned on a future. I...I knew he was going to school and that I would return to my home here."

"And he knows nothing of this?" Naomi stared at her. "How could that be? This Brock has no idea that he will have a son or *Dochder*?"

"Naomi, this isn't his situation. He doesn't have a *Boppli*," Lydia lifted her gaze to steadily meet her sister's. "This is my *Boppli*, mine and Daniel's. It will be raised in our world and will follow *Gott's* direction." There had been no movement from the *Boppli* all during her time with Naomi, but now as if the name of her husband had woken it, the babe now chose to move inside her. Lydia pressed her hand to her body.

"But it is a child of this *Englischer's* seed," Naomi insisted in a lowered voice. "I cannot see how he could lie with you and not consider this eventuality."

Making herself act naturally despite the fluttering low in her body, Lydia went on tacking a sleeve into the shirt she held. "*Neh*, Naomi. You forget that the *Englischers* use things to block conceiving. They lie together without even thinking of this outcome. We, of course, do not take these drugs, but I've thought about this a lot. I don't think it occurred to Brock to question whether I, too, was taking this birth control. Our ways are so different from those of *Englischers*."

The shirt her sister was sewing again settled unattended into her lap. "Then…"

"*Yah*," Lydia interrupted, shame staining her cheeks, "it was me, Naomi. I was careless and stupid. I should never have allowed myself to…but I was alone there and…and foolish."

She stopped to brush away the dampness on her cheek, hoping her sadness and guilt didn't seep into the child. "It does no good to talk of this. I have prayed and prayed. I believe in my repentance that *Gott* forgives me, but I still must deal with the earthly consequences of my sin."

"This is true." Naomi started again plying her needle, looking up to say, "but, *Schweschder*, have you not considered that this Brock has a—a right to at least know?"

"What do you mean?" Lydia stared at her.

"Only that the *Boppli* growing inside you is his also. Of his seed." Naomi flashed a glance at her before looking back at her sewing. "It seems as if he has a right to know of it."

Staring ahead without seeing, Lydia grappled with what her sister said. The thought that Brock might care or wish to know about the *Boppli* simply hadn't occurred to her.

Daniel had pressed his hand so reverently against her to feel the *Boppli's* kick. In all his speech and all his actions, he claimed the child as his own. The thought of denying his claim now made her shudder a little.

She shook her head. "*Neh*, Naomi, I can't imagine. As I said, *Englischers* take something to keep from conceiving and often do something to stop *Bopplis* from coming, even after conception. *Neh*, this is not something to tell Brock. He would not care about the *Boppli*. Daniel and I will raise our child."

"You do not know what he would want, this Brock." Her sister's face took on a mulish expression. "Not all men want to be kept out of this kind of situation. I believe even *Englischers* sometimes fight for their *Kinder*. He has a right to know, at least."

Lydia felt increasingly flustered as she forced out the question. "To know what?"

"That he will have a child, silly." Naomi drew her needle out of the shirt.

"You think I should—you think I should contact him and tell him this?" She gasped out the question, still shocked at the thought that Brock would care whether or not she was to have a child.

Her sister nodded decisively. "I do think this. Who knows what Daniel will truly be like with another man's child? What if he married you just to right himself in the eyes of the church and the people here?"

"*Neh*. Daniel has repented of his mistakes," Lydia responded automatically in an irritated voice. "He is forgiven and has rejoined the church. Do not withhold forgiveness."

"*Yah*. He's gotten what he wants from this marriage. A *Frau* in the church has married him." Naomi nodded wisely. "Who's to say he'll hold up his end with you, however? The father of this *Boppli* deserves to know of its existence and you, you deserve better than a *Mann* who may resent your child."

Lydia swallowed, distressed at the thought that the *Mann* with whom she was coming to feel so close could actually betray her and the *Boppli*. He seemed so determined to be a *Daed* to her little *Boppli*.

"Can you be sure that this Daniel will not break your heart as he broke Mercy's? You should not keep the *Boppli* from the *Englischer* Brock."

Lydia stared at her sister, not responding in her sudden turmoil. She now recognized that she didn't know if Brock would care to be informed of her pregnancy. But what really disturbed her was the thought that Daniel might not be the kind, trustworthy *Mann* she'd thought.

…She'd been disastrously wrong in her choices before. Maybe she was wrong in about him, too.

Her *Eldre's* house was silent around her as Lydia sat at the dinner table two days later. Her pen poised over the letter paper, her thoughts skittered away from how Daniel would feel should he find out about what she was doing. And yet Naomi's words had kept revolving in her head...accompanied by her remembrance of her own poor choices before.

She drew in a deep breath and read the letter over. Saying the facts as baldly and briefly as she could, she'd told Brock about having conceived after lying with him. She told him, too, that she was now married and that her husband welcomed the child as his own.

This should give Brock an out.

Before writing, Lydia had given the matter much thought. She considered that the *Englischer* might not even respond to the information...and in many ways this would be a relief. If he didn't respond, she'd never have to confess this moment to Daniel. She'd have no idea how to do this.

She'd gone back and forth...and back and forth on whether to write at all, but had finally come to the reluctant acceptance that her *Schweschder* had a point. Telling Brock seemed most fair...and not doing so seemed like a cowardly, thievish stealing of his seed.

Upon thought, she realized that this was not information that could honestly be kept from a man.

Folding the paper with decided fingers, she shoved it into an envelope. She had no idea if it would even reach Brock since he'd moved to his school. That, too, might be a relief. At least then, she wouldn't have to face the fact that in doing the right thing with Brock, she was betraying Daniel.

Lydia sat quietly next to him as Daniel drove their buggy into the Bontreger's yard and under the bare limbs of an oak tree the Sunday of the next meeting. Along with other buggies, they parked on a flat area some yards from the *Haus* where the meeting was to be held.

Lydia's mind had been troubled ever since Naomi had spoken about the situation with her *Boppli* and even more so since writing the letter. It disquieted her that she couldn't flat out say her sister was wrong…and this was what had finally decided her to tell Brock. The letter had to be written.

And still she trembled at having done it.

She quailed at the thought of Daniel's anger if he found out what she'd done and yet, if he were wanting out of this marriage…wanting to leave again for the *Englischer* world…she'd have given him reason.

As a result of the turmoil in her chest, she knew she had been quieter with Daniel the last few days. She usually found many things to chatter to her husband about, but she'd had nothing to say on their buggy ride to the meeting. Her mind was roiling with guilt and she could find no way to speak naturally with the *Mann* whose bed she shared.

"Are you sure you're feeling up to coming?" Daniel asked now, his gaze searching her face. "Perhaps you should have stayed to rest in bed. You have been quiet this morning,"

"I am fine." She sent a brief smile his way, his kindness further lashing her guilt.

When the buggy had fully rolled to a stop and Daniel put on the brake put, Lydia started gathering her things to get out. Finishing this, she turned to the buggy door and was surprised to look up and find Daniel suddenly there to open it. He reached out to assist her down from the buggy.

"*Denki,*" she murmured, aware of the strength in his hand as she took it, bending to shake out her long skirts when she reached the ground.

Since the Bontreger house was situated above the parking area on a little hill, they had to climb up the several yards from spot where they'd parked the buggy to the porch.

"Here." Daniel reached over to take her hand again in his. "The ground is uneven."

Lydia swallowed, her hand feeling nestled in his. Glancing over at his as-usual impassive face, she followed him, a wave of guilt engulfing her as she wondered if she was wrong to doubt this *Mann* who'd done nothing, but help her, even though he sometimes wore an uncommunicative expression. It was all so confusing. Was Naomi right? Did his benefitting by helping her make Daniel untrustworthy?

If she'd have married elderly Peter, she wouldn't have these questions, but glancing over at her husband's face, she couldn't have imagined it. Marriage to Daniel—even with her churning questions—seemed so much better.

The strong tug of his hand on hers, guiding her up the slope to the Bontreger *Haus* contrasted firmly with any doubts in her head. When they arrived at the porch level, she went to the steps, acutely conscious that Daniel's hand rested on her back, propelling her gently as she climbed to stand at the door, waiting behind an elderly *Frau*. He kept his hand on her back as they threaded through the other worshippers.

"There," he said, pointing to where Naomi sat across the room gesturing at Lydia. "I believe your *Schweschder* has a seat for you. Will you be comfortable there?"

There was indeed an empty chair next to Naomi in the already crowded room.

"I think so." Lydia glanced uncertainly at him at her shoulder. "Where will you sit?"

Scanning the full rooms, Daniel patted her shoulder. "Go on and grab that seat for yourself next to Naomi. I see a spot over by young Mark Fisher."

Spying the *scholar* off to one side, she said, "*Yah*, the *Buwe* that works with you and Abel in *Daed's* buggy shop."

"For now he does," Daniel agreed with a glimmer of a smile. "I believe his *Eldre* and Bishop Fisher will soon send him back to school full time, though."

He patted her shoulder again and the gesture had her resisting a smile. "Go ahead and sit with your sister, wife. I'll find you later."

Sidestepping along a row of chairs, Lydia settled next to Naomi, her gaze following Daniel as he crossed to sit next to Mark

Fisher. The *Buwe's* expression seemed less discontented and a smile erupted on his face as Daniel moved to sit next to him. Watching their exchange, Lydia didn't immediately hear Naomi speaking to her.

She turned. "What?"

"And the pony Apple took an apple from my hand!" Mark told Daniel with excitement. "I got even closer to him than with the carrots. I think he likes apples better."

Settling into the chair next to Bishop Fisher a few minutes later, Daniel grinned at the boy's excitement. "He must be getting used to you. Soon he will let you brush him."

Mark didn't even look like the *youngie* who sulked around Joel's shop weeks ago. "He's been letting me get closer and closer to him and yesterday I stood right next to him as Apple ate from my hand."

Daniel lent an ear to the boy's crowing, pausing to send a reassuring smile to where Lydia sat across the room.

Next to him, Bishop Fisher laid an affectionate hand on the boy's shoulder. "*Yah*, because you've showed up regular and been kind to Apple. You might remember trying this with your *Bruders*."

The *Buwe* didn't disagree, just slanting a suddenly-doubtful look at his *Grossdaddi*.

Several hours later after the sermons, Daniel, Mark and Bishop Fisher sat eating at the tables that had been crowded into the Bontreger's *Haus*. Daniel brought their conversation back to Mark's favorite subject. "I think it's very *gut* that you and Apple are growing to be friends."

"Do you think he will actually let me brush him?" Mark asked eagerly. "Maybe he'll come over when I go to his pasture."

"*Yah*." Wiping his mouth with a napkin, he recommended, "Keep visiting him regularly and Apple might let you brush him."

"*Yah*, and you could take your *Bruders* to meet the colt," the bishop agreed with a broad smile, who was seated at the table just beyond Mark. "We all need friends."

"I could take them." The boy chewed, swallowing before saying, "John and Peter would like to meet Apple."

His *Grossdaddi* nodded. "I'm sure they would. You could tell them all about learning to help the colt trust you."

Mark nodded vigorously. "I could! I'll bet that's something they've never done."

"Probably not," Bishop Fisher agreed with a smile.

Having finished his meal, Daniel got up from his spot at the table. "I must take my dirty plate to the kitchen and make room for someone else to sit here and eat this *gut* food."

"*Denki* for eating with us," the once-sullen boy called out cheerfully as he left the table.

Smiling at Mark, he stepped back to allow a *Frau* to pass.

"You're very welcome. I'm so glad we found seats."

"Me, also." Bishop Fisher smiled down at his plate, spooning up some mashed potatoes.

Waving as he left his companions, Daniel glanced around, already occupied with looking for Lydia. After the meeting, she'd helped her *Schweschder* and several other women with the Sunday meal, even though he'd been concerned this would wear her out more. Where she was now he didn't know, but he hoped she'd gotten her lunch and found a comfortable chair.

Lydia was a warm, open woman, usually honest and easy to read. It was one of the things Daniel liked about her—that trusting, friendly frankness. She'd been quiet the last day or so, however, and he could only write this down to her feeling poorly as some women sometimes did when they were pregnant.

It was strange to have someone other than himself to consider, but he found himself slipping into the job more effortlessly than he'd expected. Lydia made this easier.

The throng was thick with those still gathering or jockeying for spots at the tables as some left after finishing. He slowly filtered his way into the kitchen and—as the women who worked at the sink had no doubt stepped away for a moment—he moved over to place his used plate on the pile.

Above the kitchen sink, a window made it easier to see into the yard, across which was a barn. It was lifted to let in a drift of chilly fall breeze and Daniel hovered there, enjoying the freshness of the brisk air that sifted into the *Haus*.

As he stood in front of the sink, voices from the house's back porch filtered in through the open kitchen window. It slowly came to him that they were speaking about himself.

"How he just shows up here, acting as if he never rejected *Gott*, as if rejoining the church is a simple thing…"

He felt himself stiffening. Standing at the sink, Daniel quietly pulled his hands from under the plate he'd held. The high-pitched voice was distinctive and could only belong to one woman, the elderly wife of a nearby farmer.

Remorse sank into his midsection, like a rock. It did no good to confront this sort of whisper. He supposed only time would demonstrate his repentance.

In the midst of settling the crockery before slipping back into the other room, he stopped at the sound of Lydia's voice from outside the window.

"*Frau* Schlappach," his wife said in an usually chilly tone, "how can you speak about Daniel in this way? He has repented of his sin and been accepted into the church again. Are we not taught to forgive?"

Craning forward now to look through the window, he could hardly believe it was gentle, friendly Lydia speaking.

"Naturally, you would say that Lydia," the farmer's *Frau* said in a condescending voice. "You were somehow convinced to marry the *Mann* and I have no idea why. You're a pretty, sturdy girl. You could have chosen another. If you'd gone to a larger group, you could have had lots of choices."

"I do not know why it's so hard," Lydia responded, steel in her sweet voice, "to understand and forgive a soul who left and returned to our life. Following *Gott's* path can be difficult for us all. Are not *youngies* given a *rumspringa* to decide this very thing? This earthly life of being *Gott's* is complex and demanding."

"Well—" *Frau* Slappach started to speak.

"I cannot imagine what anyone, but Daniel would have to say about his journey," his defender interrupted to say in that same polite, steely voice. "Except to rejoice that he has once again found his way."

Daniel swallowed hard in shock. He'd never heard his Lydia speak in this tone. He would have given anything to be a fly on the back porch railing with a full view of this skirmish. Warmth started gathering in his chest.

"And as to why," Lydia said, "I married Daniel Stoltzfus, you have only to know him. To see his kind heart and gentle ways to understand. He is a strong, forgiving—as *Gott* would have us all be—and forbearing in the face of many insults. Daniel is a sweet, loving *Mann*. Is he perfect? *Neh*, but then none of us are that."

"Well—Well—" the older woman gobbled. "Really."

"I hope you have a lovely meal," Lydia said with triumphant sweetness, her form sweeping past the kitchen window.

Daniel heard the hollow sounds of footsteps on the porch and thought she must have descended to the back yard.

Feeling rooted to the spot beside the sink, he could hardly believe this furious, stinging defense had come from the woman who'd married him out of desperation and who'd sat so silent lately.

Kind, open, sweet-natured Lydia apparently had a steely side.

The warm glow that had started in his chest brightened till he felt a star was within him and it was several moments before Daniel could unclench his hand from the counter next to the sink.

Later that evening, Daniel found Lydia rocking in a chair on the back porch of her parents' *Haus*, her abstracted gaze seeming to hover in the dusk air.

"My *Frau*," he said, his hand on the porch rail as he looked up at her, "are you feeling alright? You have been unusually silent, even more than you have been the last day or two."

After a few seconds, she looked over at him. "Have I been?"

He started up the porch steps, pausing at the top as he looked at her. "*Yah*, you have. Did anything...upsetting happen at the meeting today?"

"*Neh*, not really," she shrugged. Her white *kapp* pinned neatly over brown hair, she gazed ahead over the rail in a pensive manner.

He could see keeping such things as the ugly scene with *Frau* Slappach to herself. Daniel had to admit he often decided there was no point in sharing. Hoisting himself to sit on the rail, he considered her. The sweet, graceful curve of her cheek. Her hands folded quietly in her lap. She was a comely woman, all curves in the right spots, laughing and happy and warm. It streaked through his mind that the *Englischer* boys had probably all been after her. What surprised him was that she hadn't been courting with one of the *youngies* at home. The *Menner* he'd grown up with were as blind as he had been.

"You are a *gut* woman, Lydia." Daniel tilted his head as he looked at her.

She snorted gently, her mouth wry. "We wouldn't be man and wife, if that were always the case."

"Well," he responded, "if so, I'd have then been very, very unlucky."

Lydia glanced at him, her expression considering.

Not waiting for her to speak, Daniel said, "I've been thinking, wife. Perhaps we should call the *Boppli* Matthew—since he will be a gift from *Gott*."

The corner of her mouth lifted. "You are so sure this is a boy child?"

"Maybe not," he admitted, grinning. "Although if we have a girl child we can name her *Mettabel* to indicate she's *Gott's* favor to us."

His quick response surprised a laugh from Lydia. "Then husband, you will be the one to teach your *Dochder* to spell her name…and explain to her why we named her that."

The sound of her laughter made him smile and Daniel said, "I saw you with Anna Lehmann at the service this morning. Talking more sewing."

"*Yah,* did you see us? *Neh,* not sewing talk this time."

"You have been kind to her." He dropped to the porch deck, his back against the rail as he considered her. "Having her over to help with your dress and all before we married."

Lydia shrugged, a smile crossing her face. "She is a *gut* girl in a strange town. I like Anna."

"She only has a *Mamm*? I think you said her *Daed* is no longer with us." He broke off a frond of the bush growing on the other side of the rail.

"*Neh* and there are no *Menner* in Mannheim that interest Anna." His wife continued gently rocking the chair.

"Well, I say again, you have been kind to her." Even though she'd not been well, just having Lydia sleep next to him in the little room next to her *Daed's* buggy shop made the place feel like home. He felt content with her.

She more and more felt like his rib, sewn into her by *Gott*. Daniel felt every day that he couldn't have looked ahead with such hope without Lydia's support.

CHAPTER NINE

Looking out at the drifting snow, Lydia said to her *Mamm*. "It is so pretty outside. Thankfully it's not as deep as it has been. I'm getting tired of winter."

"It looks as if the sun is trying to come out." Miriam continued placidly patting the bread dough into loaves.

Bending to open the heavy oven door, Lydia carefully slid out two pans, the bread in them risen to a steamy glistening curve that filled the kitchen with a yummy smell.

"Your *Daed* and Daniel don't even have the *Buwe*, Mark Fisher, to help them this morning since neither Abel nor he have come yet."

"Maybe they've had to do something at home and will come later."

Looking out the kitchen window at the snowy yard with little white drifts up the buggy shop walls, Lydia commented, "Even though it only snowed a little during the night, I'm glad the wood stove in the shop is lit."

Her *Mamm* glanced out the window. "*Yah*, let us hope it's giving off enough heat to keep their fingers warm enough to work."

A chuckle slipped though Lydia's lips. "Of course, we want them to be able to keep working. That would be the most important thing."

"Your *Daed* certainly thinks that, given the number of buggy orders he's gotten recently. His reputation as a buggy builder has brought buyers from other areas." Miriam complacently shifted the new rolls of dough into clean bread pans waiting nearby. Glancing over after completing this task, she said, "You and Daniel can sleep in one of our bedrooms on colder nights, you know. I meant to tell you this yesterday. Your room probably gets chilly."

Flushing at the thought of sharing a bed with Daniel in her *Eldre's* home, Lydia took the bread pans her *Mamm* had just loaded and bent to place them into the radiant stove. She nudged the pans back on the oven shelves. Bending was more and more awkward as her midsection thickened, but chores still needed to be done.

"*Denki, Mamm*, but it's been just fine. With the stove, we're not cold."

She'd been sleeping in Daniel's bed since their marriage, but that nearness to him felt less and less awkward. The nearness of his warmth had grown more familiar, but she shied away from performing such a simple act under her *Eldre's* roof. It just felt…strange somehow.

"I think our room being snuggled next to the buggy shop helps, *Mamm*. It's near the barn with the horses, too, and is warmer there than outside, I think." Even with her reluctance to take her mother up on the offer of their extra bedroom, Miriam's concern warmed Lydia. She knew her *Mamm* liked Daniel, but she wasn't so sure of Miriam's opinion of Lydia's having married him, instead of following Miriam's advice to give her *Boppli* to Cousin Rachel.

Just then the kitchen door blew open with a suddenly spring-like gust as Daniel came in, pressing his back to close it behind him.

"Your *Daed* and I need your help, Lydia." His words were abrupt.

Having turned rosy cheeks away from the warmth of the oven at the sound of the opening door, apprehension flashed through Lydia at the tense note in Daniel's voice.

"What's wrong?" Miriam spoke anxious words that only echoed the streak of concern that went through Lydia.

"Joel and I took the big buggy we've been working on out for a test ride. It skidded off the mud-lick road with him. I managed to jump clear, but your *Daed* landed wrong on his leg. We need your help. I've already been to the Yoder farm—the only one close by—only all the *Menner* are away and I don't want to leave Joel injured in the wet cold."

Lydia took a step forward. *"Daed's* hurt?"

He put out a cautioning hand. "He's okay, but he wrenched his leg when he jumped clear of the sliding buggy and he can't walk on it. I moved him to the road before I came back on the horse. Joel's okay for now, but I need some help to get him back here. I'll have to go back to get the big buggy after we bring him home since we can't leave it there."

Yanking a thick coat from a peg by the door, Miriam said, "Take me to him."

"Yah. Can you get your smaller buggy for him? I think it will jolt Joel less. He's tough, but I think it'll be less painful." Daniel asked over his shoulder before he turned back to Lydia. "After your *Mamm* and I take care of your *Daed*, I'll go back to get the buggy out of the ditch. I may need your help. Our recent snowy rains have made the ground soft and mushy."

"I'm coming with you now to get him. Then we can go back for the big buggy." Lydia scooted past him, grabbing a winter jacket from the peg as she followed her *Mamm* out the door.

"You'll get wet and chilled!" Daniel protested, following her down the porch steps.

"I'm fine," she retorted. "Do you think this is the first buggy I've helped *Daed* get back on the road?"

"Or the first time he's hurt himself in this work?" Miriam added wryly as she seated herself in the narrow box of the buggy he had waiting outside.

Daniel quickly harnessed the horse Lydia grabbed from the pen near the barn.

"You and your *Mamm* are strong-minded women," he commented, reaching over to tuck a lap blanket over Lydia before starting the buggy off.

"Like she said," Lydia stuck her hands under her thighs to keep warm, "this isn't the first time *Daed's* had a buggy slide off the road. It happens."

"I suppose so."

Out of the corner of her eye, Lydia saw him smile as he shook his head.

"Okay." An hour later, from where he stood at the bottom of the boggy, snowy ditch, Daniel called up to Lydia at the edge of the country road above. "I have the ropes attached to the horse harness up there and secured now to the buggy down here. You need to slap the horse's rump to get it moving. Make sure you can get out of the horse's way. We don't need you knocked over."

Having gotten Joel Troyer comfortably ensconced in a warm chair at the *Haus* with *Frau* Troyer fluttering around to prop the older *Mann's* ankle, Daniel now focused on getting the big buggy they'd been testing back up on the snowy, muddy road.

At the farmhouse, Lydia had given him a stubborn look and informed him she was coming with him to help.

Thank heaven it was warming and he didn't wasn't worried that she would freeze out here standing on the road.

"Okay." Lydia looked down at him, snow melting from the grass around her feet at the road's edge. "I'll do that then I'll be right down to help you push."

Daniel's head slewed up quickly to look at her. "What? *Neh.* You stay there at the top! Stay there. Stay."

Turning back to the buggy, he heard her yell back with laughter in her words, "Woof, Woof!"

He couldn't help grinning, shaking his head at her dog impression as he braced his arms on the back of the big buggy. The melting snow in the ditch left him standing in muddy grass and his shoes squelched as he shifted his feet to a better pushing position.

"Shall I use my paws to pull the ropes when you push?" She called down, her lovely face peering at him from the road.

"*Neh*, don't pull, just steer it up." Daniel grinned at her, settling his feet more securely as he prepared to heave the buggy up the hill.

"I think it's getting warmer out here," Lydia called to him. "The wind has dropped off and the sun is coming out. It's almost too warm in this jacket. Of course, the warmth is making the road messier."

"Yes, it is," he muttered to himself as he leaned against the buggy, expecting it to roll forward some. "Do you have hold of the traces?"

"I do!"

Leaning in again, Daniel felt a little movement, but not much. The mud at his feet made another squishing sound with his shift.

"Remember. Don't pull on the ropes. I don't want you straining," he cautioned her loudly, gritting his teeth as he shoved again.

She made a scoffing sound. "I'm fine."

Looking up just then, Daniel saw her glance down at herself with a chuckle as she said, "Just a little thicker around the middle."

He didn't bother to reply.

After another fifteen minutes of shoving, Daniel stood to rest a moment, panting. "This is maddening! I get it so close to moving and then it rocks back."

"You need assistance."

He looked up at the sound of Lydia's words to see her coming down the slope toward him. "What are you doing down here?"

Continuing to tromp carefully along the steep grassy slope through the remaining patches of wet snow, she grinned. "Coming to help. Don't worry. I tied the buggy rope to a branch. It's out of the way and won't get tangled as we bring the buggy up, but I think we'll get further if we both push."

She lifted her feet more as she got to the bottom of the ditch. "Wow. It's really boggy down here now."

"*Yah*, you see why you shouldn't be here," he said. "Water from the melting snow is softening the ground."

"This is fine." Her reply was given in an airy tone. "I've had to deal with much worse, helping *Daed* in the past.

The thought of Joel stilled Daniel's tongue. He should probably have sent her back up to the road, out of any range of a problem, but he had to admit to being stumped by the situation.

Lydia slogged the rest of the way over through the wet grass to stand with him at the back of the buggy. "Let's both push."

Looking at her doubtfully, he couldn't think her pushing with him would do much good. Still, when she purposefully leaned her weight against the back of the buggy a fraction before he gave the buggy a shove, the black frame seemed to shift a little.

"Wait!" He hurriedly thrust his shoulder more firmly against the back of the black buggy. "Now again."

Throwing all his weight against the mired buggy, Daniel felt it shift forward a fraction more before it rolled back. He straightened, telling Lydia beside him, "Maybe it we shove it again for a longer moment—"

Beside him, having moved her one shoe in the muddy grass, he saw Lydia lift her knee to pull again on the other foot before a startled look crossed her face at the resultant sucking sound…and she suddenly lost her balance, falling backward toward the long wet grass, windmilling out with her arms.

"*Aeeeeiiii!*" Lydia's squeal sounded as she tilted backwards in almost slow motion.

Lunging forward to catch her hand, Daniel felt the catch of her grasp, tilting him off balance as well. He tipped forward, following her as she slid backwards into the muddy ditch with him falling over her. Only his braced arms kept his weight from landing on Lydia. Twisting his body in mid-fall to land on his braced arms to make sure he didn't slam into her, he felt the cold, wet grass come up toward him at the same moment he heard her squeal cut short by a gasp.

They landed—her backside on the soft ground and him bent over her in an arch and they froze there for a second. Their sudden stop with him poised over Lydia surprised a laugh out of Daniel.

Collapsing next to her in the mud a moment, he quickly gasped out. "Are you alright? Did you hurt yourself?"

Shoving a hand at her muddied white *kapp* that had shifted askew, she giggled and took a moment to assure him. "*Yah*. We're fine, the *Boppli* and me. When you grabbed me, you slowed down my fall."

Squirming in the mud, she said, "And I think the grass here is pretty thick, too. It cushioned us."

"I'm glad," Daniel said, still surveying their positions as the damp seeped into his pants. He squirmed. "Although I'm not sure we'll ever be able to get the mud stain out of our clothes."

Sprawled in the muddy, grassy ditch next to him, Lydia started to giggle.

"What?" he demanded, stopping in his clearly futile act of trying to rub the dirt off his hands. "You think this is funny, woman?"

"I'm sorry!!" Lydia shook with unsuppressed laughter. "It kinda is! You should see yourself!"

His broad hat having fallen onto the wet grass next to him as he fell forward, he felt his sweat-dampened hair clinging to his head, heat still rising from him after his strenuous pushing at the ditched buggy.

A reluctant smile slowly lifted the corner of his mouth. "I suppose I do look rather messy."

Laughter wailed from Lydia, now doubled over with her mirth as she gave way to the giggling. "You—you look—won—wonderful!"

"Except," she straightened, still wheezing with spasmodic laughter as she brought a handful of mud down on his head, "a little too clean!"

Daniel sat looking at her in shock, mud dribbling down the side of his face. "What? What was that?"

Shaking with new gales of laughter and not even trying to right herself in the muddy grass, Lydia was clearly gone. She lay next to him in the wet grass, quivering with laughter.

The seat of his pants wet from the grass and his now-open shirt collar revealing a sweaty neck, he still felt a little stunned at the mud now trickling down his neck, even as her laughter brought a responding quiver to the corner of his mouth.

"Woman!" Wiping at the brown water dripping off his eye brow, he looked at her. "What are you doing?"

Now rolling with laughter, Lydia wailed from the depths of the damp tufted grass, "You just looked too clean!"

Not even fully aware that his own fingers were curling in the mud, he found himself shaking droplets of muddy water at her…and then he stopped. He'd never wanted to kiss Lydia more.

Suddenly leaning forward, cupping a grimy hand under her muddy chin and slanted his mouth across hers. She was warm and sweet, her lips trembling briefly under his and Daniel lost another piece of his heart to her in that moment.

He didn't know how he deserved the blessing she was to him.

"You have been *gut* for Mark," Bishop Fisher commented, adjusting himself more comfortably on the barrel in the buggy shop later that day as the winter dusk set in. "You are a *gut Mann*, Daniel. You need to be less hard on yourself."

Sitting beside the bishop on another empty barrel, Daniel looked ahead at the big muddied wagon he and Lydia had finally dragged up from the ditch earlier.

"*Neh*. It was *Gott's* work. I merely tried to keep out of His way. Mark is a fine *Buwe*. He just needed to sort out some things. Apple loves him now."

Bishop Fisher turned toward him, the older *Mann's* expression deadpan as he lifted his brows. "*Yah*, Mark needed to sort things out as did you. That's why I thought you were the best to help Mark."

"One big difference, Bishop. My 'sorting out' hurt others." There were nights—lying next to a sleeping Lydia—after a long day helping Joel in the buggy shop, that Daniel worried he was happier than he deserved to be.

Their kiss in the muddy grass hours earlier left not only a heated glow in his body, but the joyful sense of their happy union.

"My boy, I think you make too much of your transgression, particularly now that you've returned to a godly life." Bishop Fisher's tone was laconic.

Feeling the *Mann* didn't regard his transgression as badly as he should, Daniel protested. "I-I abandoned Mercy. I upset all those here in the community and I distressed my *Eldre*. Of course, I hurt others."

"My Daniel," Bishop Fisher leaned over to press a hand on Daniel's knee. "Mercy has found the right *Mann* for her in Isaac. This might not have happened if you hadn't left the church for a while. The church members are now recovering from their reactions to your learning and...and your *Eldre* have lessons of their own to learn. *Gott* is with them."

Daniel said nothing. He still didn't know what to make of the sudden flush of heat he'd felt toward Lydia, stronger than he'd ever felt toward Mercy or any other woman. How he could deserve such a mate as Lydia, he didn't know. Sure, they were married now and she slept beside him every night...but he wasn't supposed to like it—or her—so much.

Repentance wasn't supposed to be enjoyable. Was it?

Sitting on the bed in their small room later that afternoon, Lydia buried her face in her hands. Having immediately changed out of the wet, muddy clothes she'd worn, she sank now onto the bed. She could no longer doubt that she had fallen in love with her husband...and to fear his reaction to her writing to the *Englischer*.

After they'd gathered themselves from their muddy embrace at the bottom of the ditch, they had together winched the big buggy out of the ditch and brought it here to the shop. He'd sent her to their room to change into warm, dry clothes while he looked over the damaged buggy.

She loved him.

Loved the furrow between his brows as he considered a problem like getting the buggy back onto the road, loved that he worried so much about her *Daed's* and her own well-being. Loved that he'd promised to raise the *Boppli* as his own. Even while she'd let Naomi's doubts about his commitment to her make her waver, she recognized now that she could never doubt his love for their child.

As she'd walked back to their room, she'd seen Bishop Fisher drive up, so she supposed Daniel was chatting with him now.

How could she have questioned whether her husband would see her having contacting Brock as a betrayal? Over and over, he'd spoken of the *Boppli* as their child and yet she'd doubted him. She'd allowed her fear to be prompted by Naomi's words. She could only conclude that her questions lie in whether she was worthy of being forgiven—despite her conviction that *Gott* did just that—and therefore not likely to earn Daniel's true love.

Lydia concluded that she never should have written to Brock. The turmoil in her chest seemed too big to overcome and she had an urge to go out to confess what she'd done to both Daniel and the Bishop…but she couldn't. She just couldn't make herself utter the words.

She loved Daniel too much to lose him now.

A week later a brisk, spring-like breeze blew outside the shop as she and Naomi were alone inside doing their usual yearly inventory of the shelves at the back corner of the work area. Bolts of heavy black fabric for covering buggy seats were stacked up to the ceiling, tilted on the shelves that sat in the shadows.

Lydia held the ledger in which they kept record of the number and kinds of seat coverings.

Looking back at her, Naomi abruptly asked, "What did Daniel say about you writing to tell the *Englischer* about the *Boppli*?"

The buggy shop pot belly stove hissed and popped in the silence that followed her sister's question. Not saying anything initially, Lydia only shivered in response, despite the warmth of her ever-growing belly.

"*Schweschder*, what did he say?" Naomi repeated emphatically. "He must have had some response. Was Daniel relieved that you wrote to tell this Brock of the coming *Boppli*? I always thought he'd regret agreeing to raise an *Englischer* child."

Even as her sister spoke her self-satisfied words, Lydia suddenly became aware of a chilly draft filtering into the shop corner where they stood. Looking back over her shoulder to find the source of this cold air, she saw with a shock that the main door stood ajar now...and that Daniel stood in the open door.

As Naomi's voice was clear and carrying, Lydia didn't need the thunderstruck look on Daniel's face to know he'd heard everything her sister said.

"*Schweschder*," an oblivious Naomi said again, finally looking away from her counting of the fabric bolts on the shelves, "what did Daniel—"

Lydia could almost hear her sister's swallow as she looked between them, clearly realizing the situation.

Neither sister said anything, the breath seeming to vanish from Lydia's lungs as Daniel walked slowly across the shop to them. Even the normally undaunted Naomi's words seem to have dried on her tongue.

The leather of his shoes made his steps echo in the quiet shop.

Finally, he stopped in front of them. Taking his broad hat from his head, Daniel looked down at the floor before lifting his gaze to Lydia's. "You...you wrote the *Englischer* about our *Boppli*?"

Feeling frozen to the spot where she stood with the ledger still clutched in her nerveless hands, Lydia could only stare at him with beseeching eyes, wondering how she could have been so insane as to not recognize at the time what a breach her action would seem to him.

"Now, Daniel," Naomi hurried into speak, her tone almost condescending, "you know Lydia had no choice but to inform the *Englischer* of—"

Until now, Daniel hadn't even looked toward Naomi. His voice now sliced into her words, his gaze still locked on Lydia. "Inform him of what? Of the consequences of spilling his seed without thought or concern? Inform him of how this has upended Lydia's life?"

As Naomi gobbled out an incoherent response in her own defense, Daniel shot an icy glance her way before saying to Lydia. "I think, my *Frau*, that we can do without your *Schweschder's* participation in this conversation. We are best discussing this, just you and I."

Still emitting half-sentences, Naomi could be understood to say she wasn't deserting Lydia.

Daniel's expression grew more sardonic.

"Despite your feelings about this, Naomi, Lydia is my wife." He laid awful, heavy emphasis on the last word.

While she had little defense for her own behavior in writing to Brock without talking first to Daniel, Lydia instantly flew to her sister's protection.

Tossing the ledger onto a nearby shelf, she said hotly, "Don't be mean to Naomi. She's only trying to protect me!"

His expression growing even colder, Daniel responded, "From me, I assume?"

Repressing her urge to quail under his icy gaze, Lydia stiffened her backbone. She might not have much defense regarding the letter, but she had no problem standing up for her little sister. "Naomi only has concern for me and the *Boppli*. She pointed out that you've not got the best record—"

Her words dwindling away as the lingering anger leeched out of her husband's face, Lydia fell silent, a terrible sense of tragedy filling the echoing shop.

"Of course," Daniel said eventually in a flat tone, "I am not to be trusted…so naturally your *Schweschder* questions your safety with me."

Lydia felt swept with a vast grief and anger all at once. Whirling around, she told Naomi, "You should leave. Daniel and I need to talk about this. Alone"

"But Lydia," her sister responded in a lowered voice, "I cannot just leave you like—"

"Yes, you can," she interrupted. "I am fine. Daniel and I just need to talk."

She glanced over at her stone-faced husband. "We should have talked about this before. Go on home."

When Naomi showed sign of hesitating, Lydia gave her shoulder a little shove.

"Go on. I am fine." She looked over at Daniel and said in a slightly louder voice, "I am fine. Daniel only wants what is best for me and the *Boppli*. Go."

Escorting her reluctant sister out of the buggy shop, Lydia turned back to see Daniel engaged in the mundane task of working on a buggy, his sleeves rolled up. His face set.

She hadn't lived these last weeks with Daniel not to have learned a few things. Turning, she went into their room and started lunch. There was no denying that this was a big deal. In their short marriage, they'd never argued and she wasn't looking forward to doing so now.

On the other hand, she hadn't tried to hurt him. Not deliberately.

Daniel fumed all through lunch. He sat at the small table in their room, eating in silence the delicious soup Lydia had made. The thought that he must have done something to make her doubt him kept spinning round his head. He just didn't know what.

It all seemed to come back to that miserable choice he'd made of leaving their life...

Finally, after twenty minutes of excruciating politeness, Lydia burst out from across the table, "Oh, for heaven's sake, let's talk about this."

"What do you want to discuss?" He heard the chilly sound of his voice and hated it, but dammit, he was… He was angry and… hurt.

Lydia spread her fingers out on the table cloth, saying in a deliberate voice, "I'm sorry I didn't talk with you about this. I should have done that before I ever wrote anything to Brock. I was wrong. I see that clearly now."

"That is the *Englischer*? You said his name before…Brock?"

"Yes." She responded with asperity, lifting her brows as she rolled her eyes in what appeared to be frustration.

He didn't know what she was upset about. He was the wronged one here—if a husband who wasn't trusted could be wronged.

"It just that after talking about it—" she darted a glance his way, "—only with Naomi, mind. Well, it only seemed fair to let him know about the *Boppli*."

"Fair?" Daniel stared at her angrily. "What do you mean—fair? The *Englischer* left you in a terrible way. He wasn't worried about being fair. There was nothing in this that's fair to you and yet you're worried about being just to him? I don't see that you've done him any wrong. What if you hadn't found a *Mann* to marry? You might have had to give the precious *Boppli* to your *Aenti*!"

Resting her hand on her growing stomach, she swallowed visibly before responding. "It is *Gott's* way for us to be kind to others, *yah*? Being fair in this isn't truly about Brock, but about me living as the faithful servant *Gott* desires us to be."

She paused, visibly trying to speak calmly, "I have already sinned, Daniel. I put myself and the *Boppli* at great risk in doing so… I don't want to again—to again react without thought."

"And yet you thought I had no right to be part of this decision? This major decision about our child?"

She didn't meet his gaze. "I said I'm sorry. I should have spoken with you about it, of course. I see that now."

Staring at her with a thousand thoughts racing through his brain, he took a moment before responding. No matter what she said, he knew why she—and the others—hesitated to trust him.

"Lydia, I-I made a disastrous decision. I rejected *Gott* and our *gut* life here. I can see my own blame, why you and your *Schweschder* do not trust me. Your stain is so much smaller than mine."

"It's not that!"

"I know that you also made not the best choice for you when you were with the *Englischer*. It was not a rejection of *Gott*, though. I do not see that you owe this *Englischer* anything." His soup long forgotten, he found his hand clenching into a fist on the table. "I told you when we made the plan to marry that this is now my child—my *Boppli*. The *Englischer* has no right to him."

Tears filled Lydia's eyes and she burst out, saying, "This is why I didn't tell you! I knew you'd be upset and...and not want me to write him. Don't you understand? I could not *not* do this...and yet you are angry about it!"

Daniel could only look at her in frustrated silence as she wiped the moisture away from the corners of her brown eyes. After a few minutes, he said, "I'm sorry that you have been in such an uncomfortable dilemma. But this *Boppli* is now my child. Mine, too. Even though I am an unworthy *Mann*, I wish to be a *gut Daed* to it. I love this *Boppli*. I want to...to be a different *Daed* to it than..."

"—than you had," Lydia finished when his words dwindled away. "I'm sorry, Daniel. Our marriage has been a gift and I never wanted you to feel I see it any other way. I—I don't think Brock will want the child. I'm not even sure the letter will reach him."

Daniel stared at her across the narrow table, wrestling with his own culpability. What right did he have to chastise her about anything? If nothing else, her action stressed again how unworthy he was.

Reaching out her hand, she grasped his. "There is nothing for either myself or the *Boppli* with Brock. I promise. I was...just doing what I thought I should do. Please believe me."

That was the problem, he thought in silence. He wasn't sure he had any right to expect trust from her. He, who out of his own pride and fear, had broken the deepest trust.

Days later, Daniel walked up the gentle sloping drive toward the buggy shop, a chilling, spring drizzle soaking him through as it fell all around him. He walked on through the sheets of rain, brooding as the wet clung to his jacket, soaking his shoes and the bottoms of his pants. Only his broad work hat shielded the droplets from landing on his face.

He and Lydia had gone through the motions of daily life since he learned about her having sent the letter and, although the knot of betrayal in his chest had loosened some, it was still there. He heard what she'd said, that she'd felt she'd had to let the *Englischer* know, but he couldn't dismiss that she was rejecting his ability to father the child. He knew he'd sinned beyond forgiveness for many.

Even when she'd curled beside him in her sleep, he'd made himself turn away. Even though he was bruised inside, even though he had no right to any consideration, he still felt she'd betrayed him.

Never having let his face reflect his inner troubles, he doubted Joel and Miriam had any idea of their quarrel, unless Lydia had spoken of this to them.

An image of her that morning, sewing small clothes at their table after she'd cleaned up from breakfast, shimmered briefly before his mind's eye. Her waist thickened with the coming *Boppli*, the sweet curve of her cheek as she bent forward. This whole matter of her betrayal wouldn't have hit him so hard, if he hadn't fallen so hopelessly in love with his own wife.

The ground beneath his feet leveled off as he got closer to the Troyer *Haus*, positioned conveniently across the back yard from the buggy shop. The dirt of the drive soaked from the cold, steady rain, his feet squished to a stop.

An *Englischer* car was parked between the two buildings, its garish red paint splashed with mud. Shifting his gaze from it after a moment, Daniel felt a bolt of shock run through him. There on the back porch of the *Haus* was his pregnant Lydia—her white *kapp* proclaiming the commitment she'd made to him—talking in an animated way to an *Englischer Mann*.

The *Englischer* who was even now touching her.

The streak of heat that had hurtled through him at the sight of that *Englischer* with his hand on Lydia's arm was quickly followed by a blast of bone-deep cold, his blood feeling like slush. Frozen in place at the edge of the drive, Daniel felt for the first time the urge to take a *Mann* by the neck and squeeze the life out of him.

This had to be the *Englischer* Brock.

Even when at his most troubled and having run in fear from the *Englischer* world, even when Isaac had mocked him, he'd never before had the urge to kill a man. He did now.

This was the *Englischer* who'd stolen Lydia's peace. Taken her world and ripped it apart.

Daniel was torn by his conflicting urges. He wanted to bound up the porch steps and strike Brock repeatedly with his fist—beat the pulp out of him for having dared to lure a woman of *Gott* to such a situation. He felt his fingers curl into a sledgehammer.

At the same time, Daniel's brain registered that Lydia stood next to the *Mann*, not shaking off his hand, her beautiful face upraised to Brock's in earnest conversation.

It was as if she wanted to—to be with him. Wanted him to keep touching her.

The very thought sent a different urge bolting through Daniel. Maybe Lydia did want this *Mann* touching her. Maybe he wasn't unwelcomed. Maybe she'd wanted this when she'd written him.

Swallowing as the cold inside of him deepened, he wanted to turn and walk quickly back down the drive. To keep walking and running forever. He ached to run from the pain staring him in the face. To leave here…and her. Maybe she wanted this Brock to touch her, wanted to curl in bed next to him.

To have him raise her *Boppli*.

The thought—once it snuck in—bloomed into a huge evil conviction. Daniel felt the urge pulling at his feet. Leaving her with the *Englischer* just made sense.

In a faint sort of way it seemed to Daniel through the haze of his despair that this was what he'd done when faced for the first time with the frightening *Englischer* world. He'd run.

Turning away from the sight of Lydia, Daniel slogged silently down the hill through the rain.

CHAPTER TEN

Darkness brushing now at the windows of their room hours later that night with the grayness of a wet spring, Lydia bent over her stitching, trying to keep from glancing again at the door. An old wind-up clock ticked on a shelf by the small dining table. On the shelf above the wood stove was a covered plate holding Daniel's supper for when he returned. Even though she didn't know why Daniel hadn't come back to eat with them, her *Mamm* had insisted on Lydia taking him some supper.

Where was he? Was he hurt? Did he need her?

When she asked her *Daed* if he'd sent Daniel on a buggy-shop errand, all the older *Mann* could only look mystified and say was that the business he'd sent her husband on wasn't dangerous and shouldn't have taken Daniel more than the morning.

His absence niggled at her still and she stitched blindly, fearful of what might have befallen him. Things had been strained between them since he found out about her having written to Brock. She'd hated Daniel's silence and the still darkness of his blue eyes, signaling that he was clearly miles away from her.

And then there had been the surprise visit from Brock to deal with.

It all left her uneasy.

Lydia's hand resting on her now-rounded belly, she worried again that something had happened to him. She couldn't help remembering her *Daed's* recent tumble into the steep ditch that had left him lame. Fortunately, Daniel had been with him and could go for help. Was her husband even now in dire straits but had no way to cry for help?

Her marital vows meant a lot to her. She wished her actions hadn't meant otherwise to Daniel.

Putting her hand over her belly as if by thus she could convey calm to the child inside, she tried to calm her own fears. What with Brock's surprise visit here, she mused, she had so much to tell Daniel. If only he would come back—

The latch on the door clattered suddenly then, making her jump. Lydia whirled around to see him step inside.

"Oh, you startled me! Are you alright? You're so late..." In the midst of jumping up to greet him, her words dwindled to stop at the sight of his face. Icy, dark stone would have looked more welcoming.

"Daniel? Are you okay? I wondered why you...didn't come home to eat with *Mamm*, *Daed* and I." It seemed a natural thing to say, but the darkness on his face had her words stumbling to a halt.

"Did you?" he asked in that hard voice she hated. "Did you wonder?"

"*Yah*," she responded, watching him cross the room to the cabinet where his clothes were kept.

He'd opened a door and was taking out stacks of clothes. "I thought the seat next to you was taken."

"What?"

"Could the *Englischer* not stay for dinner?" He looked over his shoulder at her, the blankness on his face worse than an accusation.

"*Englischer*?" she faltered, bewildered by the rage and fury...and distance...emanating from him. "Do you...mean Brock?"

At the last word, Daniel stopped taking clothing out of the cabinet, swinging back to her. "I do not remember the *Mann's* name who took your virtue, Lydia, and left you unmarried with child, but that was he there with you today on the porch, wasn't it?"

"*Yah*," the words hurried out of her, "but only because I—"

"You summoned him here." It was a flat statement, made as he laid the pile of his clothes on a sheet, beginning to fold it over the stack. "When you wrote to him of the *Boppli*. Well, you can now leave with him."

"What!" In her wildest nightmares, she'd not expected anything like this. "But—"

"I have been at Bishop Fisher's *Haus* since seeing the sight of that *Englischer* with his hand on your arm—"

He stopped, his jaw hardening.

"Daniel, can I explain to you what you saw?" Lydia couldn't help the frustration and anger in her words.

"There is nothing to explain." He picked up the bundle. "I will be sleeping at the Bishop's tonight. You can tell your *Daed* that I'll be here to work in the shop in the morning. I'll not leave him without help during this busy time."

Her anger now mixing with a jolt of panic, she started forward toward him. "Daniel, let us talk about this. I'm not—"

"There is nothing to discuss, Lydia." For a brief flash, she thought she saw a soul-searing grief in his face, but it was quickly shuttered. "I am glad you will now have what you have wanted all along."

"After all I've done, I deserve no better," Daniel said to Bishop Fisher out by his barn the next day, a chilly spring breeze pressing their coats against them.

The two worked together, checking out the Bishop's farm equipment before the spring planting.

The older *Mann* smiled faintly. "*Lappich Buwe*, why would you say such a thing? You are a child of *Gott*. You made a mistake—which every sinner does. If He has forgiven you, why can you not forgive yourself?"

Daniel looked over, trying to ignore the roiling in his belly. "If this is not my punishment, why has it happened? She was there with him. I saw them. The *Englischer* had his hand on her arm."

The very thought of another touching her made him want to vomit.

"I am not sure why," Bishop Fisher responded, shaking the rag in the wind after he'd run it over the plough. "I am not actually sure what happened? Did you ask Lydia why the *Englischer* came? Why he touched her?"

"*Neh*," Daniel answered heavily. "I—I couldn't stay after I saw her there with him."

He'd never felt this churning inside, even when a *youngie* alone in the *Englischer* world. Not even after he'd renounced his church membership, determined to prove himself capable of making his way in that world.

"I felt—alone—and isolated after I left the church and our way of life, but this..." His words trailed off as he continued the routine task, moving on to check out the hay baler and loaders. "I am *grank. Grank.* I do not know what to do."

Swallowing hard against the tightness in his throat, he forced out the words, "I love Lydia. I think I have loved her ever since going to work for her *Daed*. I saw her then, you know?"

The older *Mann* nodded without speaking.

Daniel muttered. "I saw her. I did not only marry her to be a *Daed* to the *Boppli*, but...because of her."

After a few moments of silence, Bishop Fisher said, "I know this is troubling you sorely. When I am weighed down with burdens, I speak to *Gott*. Maybe you need to do the same."

His friend and mentor again flapped the dusty cloth in the wind before turning back to Daniel.

"You may have felt alone, *der Suh*, but you never were." Bishop Fisher smiled at him. "Pray."

Bedded down that night on Seth Fisher's couch, Daniel fought with the pillow given him, trying to find some comfortable shape to stuff under his head. Punching the innocent feather rectangle again in a desperate attempt to adjust himself for sleep, Daniel became aware of Mark, Bishop Fisher's *Kleinzoon*, peering at him over the back of the couch.

"Mark," he said by way of greeting the *Buwe* who was supposed to have gone off to bed with his cousins several hours before, "you know the cows will need to be fed and milked very early tomorrow, right?"

"*Yah.*" The boy blinked at him solemnly. "Why are you here and not in your room at Mr. Troyer's buggy shop? Did you and your *Frau* have an argument?"

Nothing had been said earlier about Daniel's presence at the *familye* meal. He knew it was natural for the older *Kinder* at least to have wondered.

Punching his pillow yet again, he said, "You'd better get to sleep."

"Is *Frau* Stolztfus mad at you?" Mark's question was solemn.

"*Neh.* Go to bed, Mark." Daniel felt weary down to his bones.

The *Buwe* continued staring over the couch.

"Would it help if you introduced *Frau* Stoltzfus to Apple? He's a very nice horse."

A reluctant smile tugged at Daniel's mouth. "I'm glad to hear it."

"I think you and *Frau* Stoltzfus will work things out. Everything will be fine."

Embers from the evening fire popped gently in the stove and Daniel just looked at Mark without reply.

"I like her. *Frau* Stoltzfus. She's a nice woman." The words seem to burst from the *Buwe*. "Even to me."

"Why shouldn't she—or anyone—be nice to you?"

"I haven't always been..." Mark ducked his head as he seemed to grapple for the right word. "I can be a *Debiel*."

The term was so unexpected that Daniel chuckled despite the sick feeling in his chest. "You're not a moron, Mark. You've just been confused."

The *Buwe* looked up with a sudden smile. "That's the same as you, isn't it? You were confused and left here, but now you've come back and married Lydia. You've been confused, too."

126

Lydia hardly slept that night, her tears drying into crusty streaks on her face. Curled in a ball in the bed she'd shared with the *Mann* she loved, she wept, whispering desperate prayers.

Dear *Gott*, she prayed, be with me. *Stay with me in this my darkest hour. I did not know what to do! This is why I wrote to Brock. Was I wrong?*

Even when unmarried and pregnant, she hadn't felt this—this despair. The child stirring within her only made her cry harder. In messing up her marriage, she'd driven the *Boppli's Daed* from him. Rejecting with no consideration at all the realization that she could summon Brock back, she rocked against her pillows, trying to console herself and the babe stirring inside her.

These last months with Daniel had been filled with a sweet gentleness. He'd been nothing, but kind to her and she outright rejected the thought that Naomi would say he probably did this out of self-interest. Her Daniel. The *Mann* who'd hung damp sheets on the line with her and tolerated her gales of laughter when the wind snapped the wet fabric across his now-beloved face.

At some point in the black night, it occurred to her that she'd once again allowed herself to be influenced. Not by an *Englischer* this time, but by the sister she loved. She couldn't blame Naomi. Her silly little *Schweschder* didn't really know Daniel, not the *Mann* Lydia had come to know.

Staring up into the dark, Lydia accepted that in her anxiety and fear, she'd let Naomi's questions infect her. Didn't *Gott* recommend them to know others by the love they showed?

She should have trusted Daniel's actions.

Early the next morning—mists still curling in lower areas— Daniel stood in front of the barn behind his childhood home. Old Rusty was standing placidly in the pale light, hitched already to the work wagon that was used in the fields.

It felt both accustomed and strange to be back here. He felt no ownership. This farm was now destined to pass on to Bart, his *Schweschder* Judith's husband. Daniel felt only a twinge at this thought. It brought back to him the reality of his own poor choices, but if Bishop Fisher—and even his *Kleinzoon,* Mark—was right, Daniel needed to move on from his regret and accept *Gott's* forgiveness.

If the truth were spoken, he felt more comfortable in Joel's buggy shop than he'd ever been in the life of a farmer. Now, with his broken marriage to Lydia, even that seemed to dangle uncertainly.

Wrenching his mind back to the moment, Daniel stood in the crisp morning air, hearing his *Daed's* rough voice mixed with Bart's as they readied to head out. He'd come here to see the old *Mann*, not even knowing what he had to say.

Last evening as he'd tried to settle himself comfortably on Bishop Fisher's sofa after Mark's visit, Daniel had found himself dwelling on Lydia's comments as they'd driven away from eating with his *Eldre.* Back then he'd dismissed her having said that his *Daed's* quietness made it difficult for Daniel to feel loved by the *Mann*, but now he wondered if his response to her comment had been a child's natural reaction. Did not all parents love their *Kinder*? Children did usually insist they were loved, even when the love was hard to see.

The rumble of Jeremiah Stoltzfus's words filtering through the brightening light, the thought passed through Daniel's head that his father was nothing like Lydia's *Daed*, Joel…

Somehow, Daniel needed to settle this thing with his *Daed* for himself—amongst all the other things he had to settle.

As he moved forward with a stomach that still felt queasy in him, Daniel reflected that at least now his relationship with his *Daed* didn't seem as earth-shattering. The situation with Lydia hovered over his every thought.

"*Daed*," he said, coming up in the brightening morning light to stand next to the farm wagon.

Jeremiah turned quickly away from Judith's husband, the older *Mann's* whiskers seemed to bristle more in his startled moment. "Daniel. You surprised me."

With an unintelligible murmur, Bart melted away from his *Daed's* side, leaving only the two *Menner* standing beside the wagon in the dim morning light.

"Why are you here so early?" Even taken unawares, his father maintained a stiffened annoyance in his face. "Do you not need to be at the buggy shop?"

Since this was typical, Daniel felt no need to address his *Daed's* crustiness. "*Neh*, not yet. Can…can we speak a moment?"

"*Yah*, but I must get out to the fields soon." The older Stoltzfus' agreement was clouded by the impatient note in his voice.

As an awkward silence settled between them, a familiar, disturbing sense of paralysis descended into Daniel's chest and he struggled to think of anything to say. How many times as a *scholar* had he sat in silence beside his *Daed*?

Driving to the fields…sitting at the fire in the home…

Always silence and this choked feeling in his throat. Having grown up with Joel and Miriam, Lydia just didn't understand.

"*Daed*," Daniel said abruptly, "you know I've always wanted you to be proud of me."

His father stared at him. "You did? I have not known this."

Daniel looked at the older *Mann*, knowing his having left their life for the *Englischer* world still left a bitter taste in his *Daed's* mouth. His jaw grew more rigid as he said stiffly. "I know I have made poor choices—"

"*Yah*." The word came roughly out of Jeremiah's mouth.

With difficulty—and conscious that his father had shifted away from him toward the farm wagon—Daniel blurted out, "I have made poor choices and, *yah*, I've always wanted you to be proud of me."

"Even," he swallowed against the hardness in his throat, "even when I so badly handled my *rumspringa*. So afraid and so…so insufficient from the start."

His father looked at Daniel in his fierce, silent way, finally demanding, "And this was our fault, your *Mamm* and me?"

"*Neh*, I did not say that. Not completely your fault anyway. I made many mistakes myself. Many." Clenching his hand, he remembered what Bishop Fisher had said the night before—and what Lydia had always insisted—that *Gott* loved him. Loved him with all his imperfections, loved him more than he could ever love himself. Daniel certainly hadn't been good at doing the best for himself.

"I always wanted you to be proud of me—even though I was a scared, inadequate younger son who you thought could never make it on my own."

Again, his father didn't respond, but his hard gaze did shift downward.

"I know I am not like you and Joseph and Abraham or even John." Daniel shook his head, feeling a faint, self-disparaging smile coast onto his mouth. "I worked with you in the fields alongside all the others, but I am not a farmer, *Daed*. I am much, much happier working on buggies at Joel's shop."

"*Gut*." His father finally grunted a response. "Your *Mamm* and I are glad you found a place."

"I know it was probably difficult for you both," Daniel said, the thought never having occurred to him. "This journey of mine has been hard on many."

"*Yah*," Jeremiah's expression didn't change, although he shifted back slightly to face his son.

Seeing this and knowing that emotional expression of any kind was not easy for his father, Daniel cleared his throat. "You and Bart are headed to the fields now."

"*Yah*." Jeremiah's glance toward the open barn door seemed automatic.

"I won't keep you much longer, *Daed*." Daniel paused. "I just wanted to say that my *youngie* pride, my foolishness before came out of—out of doubting myself. Doubting I was strong enough. That I could make it on my own. I—I stupidly thought I needed to prove myself, *Daed*. To you. To *Gott* and to our neighbors."

He glanced down at the barnyard dirt at his feet. "For the longest time now, I wished I could undue those weeks in the

Englischer world—take it all back—but I have come to recognize that screwing up and sinning is, is the way of this world. Even though it's hard to believe, *Gott* does not love me less and I should not forget that."

Jeremiah slowly shook his head, his gaze not leaving his son. "*Neh*. We should none of us forget that, Daniel. And *der Suh*—"

The older *Mann* put up a hand to shift back his hat, "I—I am proud of you. You have taken the harder road. More so than you deserve. Keep trying to believe *Gott* loves and forgives you."

Another kind of lump welled up in Daniel's throat and he cleared his throat, saying evenly. "Thank you, *Daed*. That means a lot to me."

He drew a deep breath. Now if he could only win Lydia's love...

CHAPTER ELEVEN

The next morning, Lydia sat brooding at the small table in the room she'd shared with Daniel. Perched to the side, Naomi sat on their bed.

Silence filled the room, the small wood stove in the corner emitting occasional pops along with its mild heat. Hunched forward, her elbows braced on the table, Lydia pulled back straighter, feeling the *Boppli* inside her stretching as if its tiny feet were braced against her ribs.

She felt another tear trace down her cheek, mourning the thought that although he'd have been a wonderful *Daed*, Daniel might not return to her.

After a few moments, Naomi said, "Maybe you should have married old Peter, after all."

Jumping to her feet, Lydia stalked to the window and snapped, "Don't say that. Don't ever say that."

"Okay, okay." Her *Schweschder* opened her hands, patting the air in a calming gesture.

"He was stupid and thoughtless to leave without giving me a chance to explain when he saw Brock here, but Daniel is my husband," Lydia said in an emphatic voice. Her throat clogged up as she said, "I love him. I really love him, the *Debiel*. He has done wrong by leaving, but he's done more right than wrong. I can only hope he returns."

"More right than wrong?" Naomi gasped. "When he stormed off after he thought he saw— Leaving you and the *Boppli*? How can you still stand by him, still love him when—?"

Lydia wheeled around, cutting her sister short. "Daniel isn't the one in the wrong here. Yes, he stormed off, as you put it, but I was the one who secretly contacted Brock and told him about the *Boppli* Daniel and I will welcome soon."

As if to punctuate this remark, the baby inside her kicked at Lydia's bladder. Wincing, she held back tears as she turned back to the window. "I can only pray he comes back."

"*Schweschder*," Naomi reminded her, "you wrote to this *Englischer* about having a *Boppli* after lying with him. And you did this without telling Daniel."

Lydia wheeled angrily around. "After you practically said I was robbing Brock if I didn't write!"

"I never said you shouldn't tell Daniel about it, though," Naomi returned in an irritating pious tone.

"No," shot back Lydia furiously, "you just now said that I ought never to have married him, but old Peter, instead."

For a long moment, her younger sister met Lydia's angry gaze with silence, broken only when she gulped softly, tears starting in her blue eyes. "I never meant you to be unhappy, sister. Truly I didn't."

Even in her distress and gripping grief, Lydia had to acknowledge that Naomi had not meant her harm. As the youngest of their family, Naomi had always been somewhat sheltered. Though guarded and spoiled by all the *Geschwischder* in their family, she'd never been mean-spirited.

Crossing the small room, Lydia put her arm around Naomi's trembling shoulders. "I know you don't want me unhappy and it was I that slipped on *rumspringa*, I who actually wrote Brock…bringing him here."

Naomi drew a shuddering breath, raising drenched bluebell eyes. "I'm sure you never thought he'd come. That was part of why you didn't tell Daniel."

"I should have, though." The sick feeling in her stomach wouldn't lift and Lydia pressed a hand to her rounded midsection, even as she shook her head. "I should have told him. He's left and I'm not sure he will return for me to tell him that the only thing I had to say to Brock was that this is our *Boppli*, mine and Daniel's, and we will raise him or her as our own. Brock is not to interfere or even visit us. If he wants to hear that the *Boppli* is doing fine, he can read the letters we will send every year or so, if he likes. After you and I talked about it, I just felt I had to tell Brock about the *Boppli*. I don't have any interest in more than that."

Gulping back her tears in an ungraceful sniff, Naomi asked, "And he agreed to this, the *Englischer*?"

"Of course," Lydia said with a wry smile. "What else could he do? He does not love me anymore than I love him. After all, he left and never planned that he and I should even meet again. I didn't, either. He actually said he knows it's best to leave the child here with us."

She left her sister's side to sink onto the bed. "I was only with Brock because I felt so lost and lonely."

Lifting her gaze to Naomi, Lydia forced out the words that had drummed in her head. "I love Daniel, though. What if—what if he never returns?"

It was dark outside later that evening when Daniel slipped the harness off Joel's old buggy horse, hanging it on a nearby peg in the barn. Situated just to the side of the buggy shop, the smallish, aged building housed several horses, the oldest of which he'd been using for an errand the day he'd returned to see Lydia with the *Englischer*.

…being touched by that *Mann*, his hand on her arm….

The heat from the stabled animals in the barn kept most of the evening chill at bay. A foggy window at the end of the row of stalls shone a spill of light from outside and the quiet of the building was filled with the faint noise of horses lipping at the straw in their feeders.

Bishop Fisher had kept reminding him that it did no good to imagine Lydia with the *Englischer Mann*, but Daniel didn't know how to stop. Images kept spilling into his head and all his prayers to *Gott* hadn't driven them away.

Lydia with that man, being touched by him, held by him.

Seeing them together—with her welcoming acceptance of the man's touch—had pictures slamming into Daniel's brain as they hadn't before. She'd lain with this man and made a baby with him.

While Daniel had, of course, known this before, it hadn't bothered him until he saw Lydia with the *Englischer*. Lydia, the woman he'd married…and fallen in love with.

Up until that moment, he'd never realized just how deeply he'd come to love his wife. His *Frau*. He suddenly felt very possessive and just the image of that *Mann's* hand on her arm still made Daniel's neck heat.

Pausing a moment now to calm himself, Daniel then went back to his task. The silence in the old barn was familiar and he recognized a silly, fondness for the place in himself. He felt a half-smile quirk the corner of his mouth.

He knew Lydia was most likely nearby. Daniel could almost hear her heartbeat from their small, shared room next to the barn or possibly up at the *Haus* with her *Eldre*. He sucked in a breath of shared air. She was here…

Unless she'd left with the *Englischer*.

Pausing as if shot through the heart by the thought—his motions of rubbing a wisp of straw over the buggy horse stopped. Maybe she wasn't here. The possibility slammed hard in his chest. Then the craziness of the thought spiraled quickly into his awareness and he again started pushing the straw over the buggy horse.

Daniel drew another deep breath as he realized that part of his agonized envisioning of Lydia welcoming the *Englischer* didn't fit.

She had returned to their life here and stayed here in Elizabethtown, even though she knew her sin would find her out. If she'd wanted the *Englischer* and that life, wouldn't Lydia have gone after the *Mann* then when she first knew about the *Boppli*?

Unless she hadn't known where to find him…, the slithering, sick feeling in his gut said.

Like a volley shot back, another thought hurtled through his brain and Daniel remembered that her letter had apparently found the *Englischer*. Lydia had known how to reach the *Mann* and hadn't before.

Who would have ever anticipated that this reality would be a relief to Daniel?

Just then the barn's smaller door jerked open, the sudden sound making him turn. The light from Daniel's lantern light shone on Lydia's rounded form. The sight of her was so beautiful that a pain shot through him at the thought of how much he loved her...and she didn't love him back.

Lifting his gaze to her briefly, Daniel then bent back over his task with the horse. Not daring to meet her gaze again, he cursed the softening in his gut as she came to him. White *kapp* over her neat brown hair, she pulled at his heart in ways he couldn't understand.

"You're home." She pulled the door closed behind her.

Her words had a breathy, anxious tone and his quick glance had told Daniel that she wore a slightly apprehensive look on her face.

"*Yah.*" Perversely—and despite the gladness in his heart that the sight of her brought—all his anger thundered back. Even though a sigh of relief went through him, Daniel's resentment and hurt took over and he said ungraciously, "As you can see, I am here."

"I'm so glad," she said, a cautious smile still on her lips. "I—I have a stew warming on the stove, if you're hungry and some green beans, as well."

His reply was clipped. "I've already eaten."

"Oh. Okay." She stood uncertainly inside the door, seeming unsure what to say.

Daniel looked over at her, the feelings rioting in his chest defying his attempts to unravel them. "I'm sleeping here tonight."

"Good." Lydia's expression seemed to lighten.

"Here. In the barn with the buggy horses." There was a strong possibility that he was being a jerk. He'd not given her a chance to tell him about the *Englischer*. Daniel didn't know if she would leave with the *Mann*, taking the *Boppli* Daniel felt was his own or if she planned to stay. He only knew that he couldn't just return to how things were between them, not with this image in his head of her and the *Englischer* she'd called to her side.

"Oh. You're…staying here in the barn." Her little welcoming smile faltered before she apparently pinned it back in place. Chin lifted, she said, "Okay. Will you be warm enough? Shall I bring you a quilt?"

Lydia's question took him by surprise. "I—*yah*, that would be *gut*, I suppose."

She could have run to Joel with this, if she hadn't already, and Daniel would be asked to leave. Only he wasn't. Lydia seemed…to accept that this was all he could give her now.

"I will bring one." She paused, half turned to leave. "I am glad you're back, Daniel. Glad you have come home."

With those words, she moved swiftly to the door and left the barn.

Daniel looked after her. He had no response to this, still a jumbled mess of heat and anger and love for her in his chest.

Three days later, Daniel grunted as he shoved a buggy wheel onto its axle. Matters between he and Lydia remained unsettled, with him still sleeping nights in the barn and working days with Joel in the buggy shop. He did not know what to do and, even though his dreams were full of Lydia and the *Boppli*, Daniel didn't know what to say to her.

Saying nothing seemed his only choice now. It was almost as if he could stave off the reality of her possibly leaving by not talking about the future.

He worked with her *Daed* every day and bed down in his lonely pallet in the barn each night. He felt obsessive, watching her belly grow rounder and rounder each day, the *Boppli's* expansion making her huff as she moved.

This uncertainty between them had to end, he knew. He was afraid to speak, though.

Just then, a clatter filled the building as across the space, Able dropped a buggy part on the concrete floor.

"Do not try to wake the dead," Daniel recommended with the quirk of a side smile. "That is *Gott's* eventual job, you know."

"I keep trying and trying to get this frame together," the younger *Mann* complained. "Maybe if you'd hold this part for me—"

"Of course." Leaving the wheel he'd been fitting on a buggy, he crossed the shop. Looking around, he asked mildly, "Has Joel left? Or is he still in the office?"

Lifting a section of wagon frame, Able grunted before gasping out, "Joel left for a moment, but he said he'd be right back. I'd like to get this piece together before he returns."

"Here. Let me fit the other side into this groove." Daniel bent to the job.

"*Denki*. That works much easier." Able straightened, the buggy shop door behind him opening to admit a burly figure.

Several packages and letters in his hands, Joel stopped beside them to remark, "*Gut*! You got that frame together."

"With Daniel's help, I finally did," Able agreed.

Having returned to his side of the shop and the buggy onto which he'd been threading a new wheel, Daniel said nothing, only acknowledging his co-worker's comment with a faint smile.

"Daniel." Joel Troyer appeared next to him, holding out an envelope. "This letter is addressed to you."

Surprised, Daniel frowned as he kept turning the axle bolts with greasy hands. "*Denki*. I have no idea who'd be writing me. Just leave it on that stool."

"Okay." The older *Mann* lay the envelope down and took his load of parcels into the office.

His face feeling tight, Daniel knew he still frowned as he wiped the axle grease from his hands. He had no idea what was in the envelope, but getting a letter was unusual. He didn't typically get mail.

With a sense of foreboding, he picked up the envelope, turning his back to the shop, to gain a little privacy.

His name and the address were printed on the envelope, obviously run through an *Englischer* printer.

Daniel unthinkingly ran his thumb over the print, his jaw suddenly tight as he clenched it. Without hesitation, he flipped over the envelope, ripping it open. The typed letter inside occupied one sheet. It whirled through his head that this could be anything. The *Englischer* could angrily be demanding the child. It could even be a paper sent by a lawyer. Although Daniel had no experience with *Englischer* lawyers, his elder *Bruder* had gotten a letter from one about a land title once. It had looked a little like this.

Turning abruptly, the paper clenched in his fist at his side, Daniel strode past where Able worked, muttering something about taking a break. He needed to be alone.

The pale spring air outside was cooling on his heated face and he crossed the courtyard behind the *Haus*, rapidly, putting long strides between him and the buggy shop. He didn't know what was in the letter the *Englischer* had written to him, but Daniel wanted no one to watch as he read what was sent.

Stopping in the field that rose on the other side of the Troyer house, he turned and sat on the damp earth, his back braced against a broad tree trunk. Below him, the *Haus* looked quiet and well-kept. From where he sat the edge of the little horse barn where he'd spent his nights recently could be seen. Coming this way had been automatic as Daniel didn't want his very-pregnant *Frau* to spy him.

Whatever the *Englischer* had to say to him could only address the heart of this.

Taking a deep breath to steady and steel his jangled nerves, Daniel sent up a prayer to *Gott* to be with him at that moment.

Still, his hands trembled as he spread open the sheets.

"Mr. Stoltzfus," the letter read, *"Thank you. When I recently came to speak with Lydia, she told me of your kindness to her. I am writing this to assure you that I heard her message loud and clear.*

Lydia told me again that neither of you want child support from me, that you married her and are fully prepared to be a father to her child. She also told me that you know that she got pregnant when we were together. I stupidly believed that like most women, she was on birth control.

Again, Lydia was very clear that despite everything she and you want nothing from me. She only wrote because she felt obligated to let me know of the child's existence. While I am fully prepared to shoulder the responsibilities of paternity—including financial support—she insisted I not do this. She was adamant that I go away and never come back. I feel wrong in doing this, as I helped create the problem, but she stressed that there is no problem as you are this child's father, not me.

I thank you, again. You are fortunate to have earned the love of such a woman."

The words swam before Daniel's eyes.

He blinked to clear his vision and looked down to see that the *Mann* had simply signed his name at the bottom of the letter. For several blank moments, he could only reread the letter, returning several times to the last line the *Englischer* wrote.

Had he? Had he with *Gott's* help actually earned Lydia's love?

CHAPTER TWELVE

Several minutes later, Daniel stared ahead into space as the single sheet of the letter crumpled in his clenched hand. Relief draining through him at the *Englischer's* indication that he intended to lay no claim to either the *Boppli* or Lydia, Daniel still didn't dare hope there was truth in what the *Mann* had written about Daniel having her love.

His jaw tightening, he knocked off his broad hat to run a hand through his hair. After all he'd done in his life, it seemed arrogant to hope that she'd come to love him as a husband. There was no denying it, though. He so wanted her love.

A brooding bleakness filled him and Daniel again felt the sting of his own loss of faith, his moments of doubt. How had he thought he had the power to prove his worth? His foolishness led him to leave the life he now recognized as the only one worth living. He'd left the church and lost sight of *Gott's* love. What made him think he was worthy? It seemed he'd done worse than the Prodigal and it still amazed him that *Gott* so loved the foolish humanity in this world.

He could only feel blessed that *Gott* had heard his cries of repentance, as Bishop Fisher assured him.

Daniel's head having dropped to stare at the dirt in front of where he squatted, he didn't immediately hear Abel calling to him.

"Daniel!! Daniel!!" The younger *Mann* came running up the hill, staggering to a stop in front of him.

Looking up, Daniel retrieved the hat he'd cast aside. His moment of private quiet was clearly at an end. Thinking he must

141

be needed in the buggy shop, he asked, "Is that undercarriage still giving you a problem?"

"No," gasped out Abel, still trying to catch his breath. "It's not that. It's Lydia. It's her time."

Daniel straightened as panic shot up his back bone. "What! She seemed fine when I saw her crossing to the *Haus* earlier. Are you sure?"

Abel just nodded, still struggling. "*Yah.* Her *Mamm* has been with her and she just now sent me to tell you to call the midwife."

Bolting down the hill to their room moments later, Daniel thrust open the door. To his great relief, Lydia's *Mamm* sat next to her.

A simple white kerchief over her hair, Lydia sat breathing through a birth pain.

Her beautiful face flushed, damp dark strands of her hair clinging to her cheek, she didn't look up as he carefully closed the door. He took off his jacket and stood quietly in respect as the only sounds in the room were the ticking of a clock on the wall and Lydia breathing as she stoically waited it out.

He remembered his own *Mamm* giving birth to his younger sister. Even though an intense experience, Rebecca had been her eighth child. This was his and Lydia's first.

He knew *Gott* had provided women with the great fortitude and love to give forth children, but Daniel's stomach still squeezed inside him.

When Lydia's pain passed and she eased back a little in the rocking chair, her *Mamm* said to him in lowered tones, "She's been at this most of the day. The pains are getting closer."

Daniel came forward and squatted beside the woman he'd come to love. He reached for the hand Lydia now rested limply on her swollen belly. "All day? Why didn't you tell me, Lydia mine? I had no idea."

Her smile was faint as she leaned against the chair's high back. "There's nothing you could do."

Reaching up to smooth her cheek with the back of his hand, he smiled tenderly. "I could be here with you."

Lydia's response was cut short as her belly visibly tightened again and she leaned forward, a frown on her face as she closed her eyes.

"You must go quickly, Daniel," Miriam urged. "Get the midwife."

Glancing up from his worried focus on his wife, he stood. "Of course. *Yah*, I will call her right away."

Grabbing his jacket off the chair where he'd tossed it, he wasted no time in finding a buggy.

Like all Amish *Menner*, Daniel had taken his *Frau* to her midwife visits, sitting beside her to hear the medical woman's instructions. He now whipped the buggy horse to a trot, knowing he had to get to the town phone box to call Rose, Lydia's midwife. If Miriam—who had herself birthed five children—said he needed to get the midwife quickly, Lydia's time was upon her.

After making the short call on the phone box outside a store, he mounted the buggy box again. The drive back to the Troyer *Haus* seemed to take forever. Daniel kept reminding himself that although it was Lydia's first birth, women did this all the time. *Gott* had given her everything she needed. Surely, she would be all right.

He believed all this, but his reminders didn't calm the jitters in his stomach or keep him from urging the buggy horse into a gallop.

For the first time he truly understood how a *Mann* could pray unceasingly…

When Daniel returned from calling Rose, he stood wavering by the door with uncharacteristic uncertainty. Almost painfully, he ached to sit next to Lydia as she dealt with this, but he couldn't be sure she wanted him there.

Then Miriam got up from the seat next to Lydia, gathering a few things to take to the small sink on the far side of the room. She stayed there, tidying things up, clearly not returning to the chair next to Lydia's rocker.

This unspoken statement of Daniel's role as Lydia's husband startled him.

Grateful for this, after a few moments, he walked over to sit in the seat next to Lydia's rocking chair.

The fact of his current estrangement from his wife and the reality that he wasn't the *Boppli's* blood father had left Daniel in a cautious, defensive uncertainty. Miriam didn't seem to feel that, at all. Her actions conveyed that Daniel had a natural role in being with the laboring woman.

The rocker was still now as Lydia bent forward. When her breathing settled back into a normal rhythm, Daniel smoothed his hand over the back of hers where she rested it on the chair arm.

She threw him a quick, strained smile as she pushed the rocker into a calming sway. "I'm glad you're here, Daniel."

He felt his throat thicken at her words. "I will always be here for you, Lydia. Do you need anything?"

"Only patience," she said, shaking her head with a wry smile. "And endurance and *Gott's* presence…and your support. Just sit with me."

The next few hours were mostly filled with silence. Miriam worked quietly on the other side of the room, busying herself with things in the kitchen area and then assisting Rose when the midwife arrived. All through the clenching pains, Daniel sat with Lydia, feeling his heart swollen in his chest. He knew children were a gift from *Gott* and he could only pray to have many more of these moments with her.

He loved Lydia more than he'd ever loved anyone. No matter what, he'd never leave her side if she wanted him there. If it took his whole life, he'd prove to her his loyalty. He wanted her to sleep next to him, to have his *Kinder* and be his *Frau* all their lives.

He recognized he was a stoic, undemonstrative *Mann* who sometimes didn't even understand himself. He certainly didn't deserve her love. Daniel couldn't imagine the *Englischer's* words were true. Lydia couldn't possibly love a man as flawed as him.

Daniel stood outside the buggy shop the next morning, the stockier figure of his friend, Bishop Fisher, beside him in the chill morning air. Having just come out of his and Lydia's room, Daniel leaned wearily against a paddock fence.

Bishop Fisher laughed, clapping a hand on his shoulder. "You have done it, *der suh*! I know Lydia and the baby boy are fine, recovering now. Are you sure you're okay?"

"I don't know." Daniel tried to ignore the moisture that prickled at the back of his eyes. "Lydia was magnificent. So quiet and contained. So beautiful."

Bishop Fisher nodded. "It is the way of women. They do this miraculous, impossible thing and look so radiant afterwards."

"*Yah*." Leaning still against the fence, he stared over the misty meadow.

"Have you and she spoken since...?" the bishop's words trailed off, his question hanging in the air.

"*Neh*, Not really. I only told her I was back and that I'd sleep in the little barn, but...but just yesterday morning I got a letter from the *Englischer*. I haven't talked to her about it."

The older *Mann* turned to stare at him. "You did? A letter? You didn't tell me. What did the *Englischer* say in it?"

Hesitating, Daniel cleared his throat. Not even to Bishop Fisher could he speak of his longing for Lydia to love him. Even if it was natural for marriages in their world to be based on love and respect, he was acutely aware that his hadn't been. If he hadn't come to work for Joel and she hadn't been in such a dire situation, would she have even considered marrying him?

"The *Englischer* thanked me for stepping in and said he wouldn't lay claim to the *Boppli*."

"That was all? This must be a relief," Bishop Fisher commented, nodding. "This, too, seems to indicate that Lydia is not leaving with him."

"Apparently not." Daniel reminded himself that her not leaving didn't mean anything about Lydia's heart. Maybe the *Englischer* hadn't asked her to join him. "I don't know—"

He broke off at the sight of a black buggy trotting down the drive toward them. The morning was still young for a random church member to come by. Sure enough, as the horse and buggy trotted closer, the thick figure of Jeremiah, Daniel's father, could be seen on the box behind the horse.

"Your *Daed*, I think." The Bishop straightened from the fence. "You will do better without me here. We will talk soon, Daniel."

With those words, the *Mann* walked to his waiting buggy as Jeremiah Stoltzfus drove up.

Feeling weary from the momentous event of the night, Daniel walked slowly toward his father.

As he got closer, Jeremiah climbed down from the buggy box, having returned the Bishop's wave as he drove away.

"Daniel!" His *Daed* greeted him. "Is it true? I heard at Bontreger's that Rose was called out to come help Lydia in the night."

"At Bontreger's store?" He himself had ridden the short distance to let Bishop Fisher know Lydia had given birth, but they'd come straight back here.

"*Yah*." Jeremiah shook his head in reproof. "The midwife, Rose's husband, came in this morning to get some things and he yammered all about it."

"Oh. *Yah*. Lydia and the *Boppli*—a *Buwe*—are inside resting." Daniel stood next to Jeremiah. The events of the evening had left him more emotional than usual, but he knew his father didn't have much tolerance for emotional words. Daniel and he hadn't ever had a heartfelt exchange.

Not knowing what to say—and robbed of his usual calm manner—Daniel just stood there, waiting for Jeremiah to speak.

The awkward quiet was broken by Jeremiah. He said roughly--in the style of a *Mann* who didn't know what to say—"You are a *Daed* now, Daniel, and I want to congratulate you. Your *Mamm* and I want to congratulate you."

Startled by these words coming from a *Mann* he'd never seen as particularly congratulatory, Daniel just nodded. "*Denki, Daed. Denki.*"

Half an hour later, Daniel stepped into the little room off the buggy shop, his stomach jumping as his gaze searched for Lydia in the bed there. Moments before, Miriam had scooted inside the buggy shop to announce that the midwife Rose had left, after cleaning up the baby and Lydia. At this news, he'd tossed his hammer on to the work bench, crossing the shop in long strides as the wheel iron he'd been working on fell to the concrete floor with a clatter.

The bedroom was warm, a gentle heat emitting from the stove, but the space smelled clean and fresh. Daniel roughly brushed at the unexpected dampness on his cheek, feeling his heart swell inside him at the sight of Lydia tucked into the white sheets on their bed with a bundle in her arms.

She looked tired now, but content against the bed pillow. When called to speak with his *Daed*, he'd left the small room shortly after the *Boppli's* birth as Rose and Miriam had bustled around. Rose weighing the *Buwe* child while Miriam assisted Lydia.

All during her labor, he'd stayed at Lydia's side, letting her grip his hands through her pains. For a smallish woman, she had quite a powerful grip.

Miriam brushed past him just then, slipping out of the room now that she'd tidied up.

Coming forward and stepping out of her way, Daniel hovered inside the door, feeling awkward and unsure. "Your *Mamm* said the midwife had left."

Lydia looked so beautiful, her brown hair now fanned out over the pillow. He swallowed hard against the lump in his throat as he sent up a prayer of thanks to *Gott*. Remembrance of the *Englischer's* letter flitted across his brain. The *Mann* cannot have known what treasure he'd relinquished, but Daniel wasn't about to tell him.

"Come in. I want you to meet your son properly." She used a finger to tuck the blanket more securely over the bundle in her arms. "Come closer."

Doing as he was bid, Daniel came to the bed, sitting down in a chair so Lydia didn't have to look up at him.

"Hello, little *Boppli*," he said softly, peering at the bundle. "He is alright? Has all his fingers and toes...and everything else?"

"*Yah*," she responded with tired contentment. "He seems very fine. Don't you, sweet *Buwe*?"

She loosened the blanket to expose the little figure in her arms. "See? All *gut*."

"He does look fine," Daniel murmured, roughly brushing at his cheek as another tear tracked silently down his face. "All *gut*."

Lydia drew a deep breath, tucking her son more securely in again. "We must talk, Daniel Stoltzfus, you and I."

Looking up from the *Boppli* in her arms, with a brimming heart Daniel said cautiously, "*Yah*?"

"You have been a *gut* husband to me." Lydia said, looking at him with a steady gaze. "Kind and loyal. Respectful and sensitive."

He didn't exactly know how to respond. He'd never been called kind and respectful before and he wasn't sure where she was going with this. "I—I have tried..."

Her next words startled him.

"I don't want you to stay here, though," she said with blunt deliberation. "Not if you're going to keep up this...this beating on yourself."

"I—" He didn't know what to say, realizing that he'd always half-expected her rejection. "Of course, if you don't want me to stay."

"Let me be clear," Lydia said, shifting to adjust herself in the bed. "I very much want you to stay and be my husband and *Daed* to our son...but only if you can do this truly. As a flawed, forgiven child of Gott, as are we all. If you can know that I love you and want you as my husband and our son's father. But only if you can forgive yourself, Daniel."

Daniel sat quiet for a moment, not speaking. "When I came back that day...and saw you with the *Englischer*—"

He swallowed, looking down at the floor. "Well, I wanted to hit him. He was...touching you. I wanted to beat him."

Looking up at Lydia, he said fiercely. "What kind of child of *Gott* is that? I know this is not the way of *Gott*. I know we are to live peaceable lives and let *Gott* deal with His children...but I could not, Lydia! I could not. That is why I left that day."

Daniel's hands clenched, remembering the *Englischer* there. Touching his Lydia.

Reaching out, Lydia stretched for his hand and he lifted it to take hers. "Daniel Stoltzfus, you are not leaving me for something like that! Brock only came here after getting my letter. He felt a responsibility, knowing I was with child. A responsibility he was only too glad to leave to you, let me add."

Still frowning, he stared down at the floor, only half believing her injunction that he wasn't to leave. "I know I am flawed, Lydia. I know you only agreed to marry me because you were in this terrible spot—"

She tugged at his hand and he looked up to see a tender smile on her face. "Isn't it said, Daniel, that *Gott* works in mysterious ways? Our little *Boppli* brought us together, but it feels very...right. Don't you *think*? Being married you and I?"

His answering smile felt fragile. "Yes, I have liked being your husband, Lydia, but the *Englischer* came—"

"And left," she responded in a matter-of-fact way, "as I told Brock he should. I don't have any desire for him in our son's life. You could never believe that, could you?"

"He was here!" Daniel bent his head again, hating that his words came out with such violence. "Here, Lydia. At your bidding."

"Not my bidding." She shook her head as he looked up. "I never asked Brock to come. As a matter of fact, I asked him to leave. I don't know what you thought you saw when Brock was here, but I want nothing from him. For myself or the *Boppli*. I wrote—oh, I wrote him perhaps because Naomi thought I should. I know I believed he should be informed that he has a—a child of his body. Perhaps he'll be more careful next time!"

Her waspish tone made Daniel smile in spite of the tearing of his heart. Clearing his throat again, he said in a thick voice, "I got a letter from him—this *Englischer*, Brock."

He looked up to meet her surprised expression.

"*Yah*, only this morning. I had no time to tell you before the baby came." Daniel drew in another deep breath. "The *Englischer* had the nerve to thank me…for calling the *Boppli* mine."

"He is yours," Lydia responded swiftly. "Our *Boppli* is yours. It could be no different."

Swallowing hard, Daniel responded by squeezing her hand in his. He could hardly see for the wetness in his eyes. "In his letter, the *Englischer* said… said that you love me. I thought he must have been wrong."

"Well, he wasn't. Not in this, anyway. I do not want you to go away," Lydia said with purpose. "I want you to stay, to love me and to have more *Bopplis* with me. And you will forgive yourself, Daniel Stoltzfus, as does *Gott*. Please forgive yourself for the mistakes you made on your *rumspringa* and after. We are all sinners on this Earth, myself included. Think what I did on my *rumspringa*. *Gott* has forgiven you as he does me. Do you think you have higher requirements of yourself than does He?"

Daniel chuckled at the thought as she tugged him forward. "I cannot see how I could have higher requirements."

He kissed her then, murmuring, "Will you help me, Lydia? Will you help me forgive myself? Be *Gott's* servant?"

"*Yah*, just as you have helped me forgive myself and accept *Gott's* forgiveness."

"I-I want to stay with you. I love you, Lydia. I want to be your husband and the *Boppli's Daed*."

"Good." She beamed a smile back at him through her tears. "*Gut*. And you can help me decide whether to call the *Boppli* Joel Jeremiah or Jeremiah Joel. I cannot decide."

Thanks so much for purchasing *Amish Princess!* If you enjoyed this book, please consider leaving a review on your favorite retailer, and look for *Amish Heartbreaker*, the next in the series!

Read on for a special look at the next in the series, Amish Heartbreakers!

Glossary of Amish Terms:

Aenti—Aunt
Bencil or Bensel—silly child
Boppli—baby
Daed—dad
Bruder—Brother
Buwe—boy
Denki—Thank you
Debiel—moron
der Suh—my son
der Vedder—my father
Dochder—daughter
Dumm hund—dumb dog
Eldre—parents
Englischer—non-Amish
Frau—wife
Geschwischder—brothers and sisters
Goedemorgen—good morning or good day
Gott—God
Grank—sick
Grossdaddi—Grandfather
Grossmammi—Grandmother
Gut—good
Haus—house
Kapp—starched white cap married females wear, black if unmarried
Kinder—children
Kleinzoon—grandson
Lappich Buwe—silly boy
Liebling—sweetheart, darling, honey
Maedel—girl
Mamm—mom
Mann—man
Menner—Men
Narrish—crazy

Neh—No
Nibling—one's siblings children
Onkle—uncle
Ordnung—the collection of regulations that govern Amish practices and behavior within a district
Rumspringa—literally "running around", used in reference to the period when Amish youth are given more freedom so that they can make an informed decision about being baptized into the Amish church.
Schaviut—rascal
Schlang—snake
Schlingel—rogue
Scholar—young, school-aged person
Schweschder—sister
Verrickt—crazy
Wunderbarr—wonderful
Yah—yes
Youngies—adolescents. Young people.

About the Author

Author Biography:

Rose Doss is an award-winning romance author. She has written twenty-seven romance novels. Her books have won numerous awards, including a final in the prestigious Romance Writers of America Golden Heart Award.

A frequent speaker at writers' groups and conferences, she has taught workshops on characterization and, creating and resolving conflict. She works full time as a therapist.

Her husband and she married when she was only nineteen and he was barely twenty-one, proving that early marriage can make it, but only if you're really lucky and persistent. They went through college and grad school together. She not only loves him still, all these years later, she still likes him—which she says is sometimes harder. They have two funny, intelligent and highly accomplished daughters. Rose loves writing and hopes you enjoy reading her work.

Amish Romances:

Amish Renegade(Amish Vows, Bk 1)
Amish Princess(Amish Vows, Bk 2)
Amish Heartbreaker(Amish Vows, Bk 3)

www.rosedoss.com
www.twitter.com - carolrose@carolrosebooks
https://www.facebook.com/carol.rose.author

Made in the USA
Middletown, DE
17 November 2020